Praise for the *Baby Shark* series

"It is rare, but magic when it happens, that a writer makes a character so real they get up and walk off the page and into your life forever. It's talent. It's Robert Fate writing Baby Shark. Kristin Van Dijk aka Baby Shark is the toughest PI in the business and Robert Fate one of the finest writers."

> — Kirk Russell, author of the John Marquez Crime Novel series

"The Baby Shark series is a high-octane pastiche of wit, wise guys, violence and thrills. Robert Fate writes noir with heart. With bootlegging, billiards, Buicks and babes, this unique series is a blue-ribbon trip down memory lane."

> — Julia Spencer-Fleming, Edgar finalist, *I Shall Not Want*

"Outboils and outwrites Dashiell Hammett--yes, Robert Fate is that good."

> — Shane Gericke, national bestselling author

"If you haven't met Baby Shark yet, now's the time. High Plains Redemption may be the best of the three."

> — Julia Pomeroy, *Cold Moon Home* and *The Dark End of Town*

"It's the transformation from what the past has made her to what Kristin can make of herself that elevates this series from your standard action shoot 'em up mystery and makes it a truly marvelous read."

> — Jenifer Nightingale, *ILoveAMysteryNewsletter.com*

"Fate has provided fans with another smash Baby Shark book. Skip work and read all day, or take tomorrow off and read all night – I dare you to try and put this book down. Highly recommended!"

> — Gregg J. Haugland *AllbooksReviews.com*

Baby Shark's
High Plains Redemption

Robert Fate

Capital Crime
PRESS

Capital Crime Press
Fort Collins, Colorado

First edition published in the United States by Capital Crime Press. Printed in Canada.
Cover art by Jack Edjourian. Cover design by Nick Zelinger.
Capital Crime Press is a registered trademark.

Library of Congress Control Number: 2008921435
ISBN 13: 978-0-9799960-2-3
ISBN 10: 0-9799960-2-3

www.capitalcrimepress.com

For Robin Bright

Acknowledgments:
My sincere appreciation for duty performed above and beyond must once again go to my compadres B.C., S.L., and G.F. Your karma is accumulating.

And special thanks to my dearest Fern, who gives and gives and gives. May your toes always be happy.

"We're turnin' to mush," he said. "We're doomed."
— Otis Millett, PI, Fort Worth, Texas

1

May 1957

MY HEADLIGHTS CAUGHT a weather-beaten sign. Curly's Tavern, the peeling paint said above an arrow that pointed to a rutted trail escaping from the road through a break in a sagging barbwire fence.

I pulled over onto the wide shoulder, engine running, headlights off, and took a look.

The building had been a farmhouse earlier in the century, set far back on a piece of property that folks in that part of the country called an acreage. Later, the farmhouse became a tavern.

The windows were blacked out. The dim light coming from the open front door barely got across the fretted wraparound porch, so I knew it didn't reach out to where I was stopped beside the road.

I could see two parked cars. Could be more behind the house. The new Buick off to the side belonged to my partner, Otis Millett.

I didn't have all the details, but what I did know was

we were doing a *quid pro quo* for a Texan named Travis Horner, whose family owned a wholesale liquor outfit. Horner's girlfriend had gotten herself into some trouble up in Oklahoma, so he called Otis. He said it wasn't kidnapping exactly, but she *was* being held against her will.

Uh huh.

He asked my partner to bring her back to him.

There were two things I didn't like about the deal. Hell, there were more than two, but first off, bagmen never get respect. And, besides that, I didn't like doing business with a two-faced bootlegger who drank his lunch with double-dealing politicians.

It was an open secret that Horner's end of the business sold booze in the dry state to our north. Whatever Otis and I—a couple of Fort Worth private investigators—were doing up there among the Sooners, my guess was it had to do with illegal booze. It didn't matter that my partner was told the job was to ransom a girlfriend.

I'd never met Horner. Otis had pointed him out to me a couple of times at the fights. That's how I knew him when I saw him: handsome, but not as good looking as he thought he was. Also, and the next I took personally, I heard he bragged about being the best pool shooter in Texas.

Anyway, my partner was going to do the actual exchange of money for the paramour. I had been called north to watch his back.

And I was late, more than two hours late, and I was sweating it.

A man came out of Curly's Tavern. Short sleeve shirt tucked into dark slacks. He carried a bag with handles.

Smaller than a doctor's bag, but that shape. He put it in the trunk of the Packard that was parked near the front steps.

After he closed the trunk lid, he fired up a cigarette and stood around smoking it.

Until he showed up, I had considered leaving my car where it was and hiking back to the tavern. Less intrusive than driving in. However, time was passing, and Otis was for sure wondering where the hell I was.

I swung my Olds 88 across the road, threw on my headlights, and began dragging bottom up the rutted driveway.

That brought the man's head around.

Through the cloud of panicked insects that led my advance up the long drive, I saw him start toward me. His fast pace made me think he wanted to meet me as far away from the tavern as possible.

I switched on my brights and took a look at him. Baby-face. Twenties. Shock of sandy hair. Light blue shirt. He frowned and shaded his eyes with one hand; with the other, he waved at me to stop, then scrambled back to keep from being run over as I drove by.

Tough weeds flapped and scratched the underside of the car as I mowed them down on my way to the side of the house. I circled around and stopped near Otis' car. I was pointed toward the highway, which again put my high beams in the eyes of Baby Face.

I cut the engine but left the lights on. I stuck the extra .38 that I carried in my purse into my belt and pushed my purse under the seat. Rummaging in the glove box, I came out with a blackjack. Then I stepped from the car and stood behind the open door.

My new leather jacket was 'cut like an Eisenhower,'

the saleslady had said. That and a light cotton blouse, Levi's, and boots made an outfit perfect for my kind of work, especially in a yard choked with weeds damp from the earlier rain.

Baby Face used one hand to shade his eyes. With the other he drew a revolver from a holster he wore on his belt.

Quick temper, quick draw.

He couldn't see crap as he marched toward my headlights and did a jerky sidestep when he flushed two jackrabbits. They ran a high-bouncing, zigzag path off into the open field that lay adjacent to the tavern property. Long, hard shadows cavorted after the hares as if they had crazy lives of their own.

His body motion said he was embarrassed by his reaction to the bunnies. "What's the matter with you?" he shouted.

He was still far enough away that shouting made sense, but his pace was closing the gap fast. I thought I heard music coming from the tavern, but given my flawed hearing from a beating that I'd taken a few years back, I could've been wrong.

"Are you fucking blind? I told you to stop!"

By that time, he was too close for that volume, but he was on a roll. He looked to be five-six or -seven, so I was a shade taller in my boots, though he was muscled up. Probably weighed in at one-fifty. He had an easy twenty pounds on me. His upper body strength was bound to be superior to mine, too, and he had a pistol in his hand.

But I had a plan.

I reached in, turned out the lights, and closed the door

as he approached the car. He blinked, trying to adjust to the sudden darkness.

I took a couple of steps to the side, away from the car, and asked in a girly voice, "Are you mad at me?" I wanted him to home in on my voice.

He was breathing hard as he tore through the wet weeds, coming straight at me. "I'm gonna slap you shit-less," he huffed, his eyes squinted.

I stepped in and whacked him above his ear with my blackjack. He grunted and gave me a wide-eyed stare before his eyes rolled back and he went down for the count. I picked up the revolver he'd dropped and flung it after the jackrabbits.

As I rounded the corner of the house, through the rough weeds and thick humidity, I *did* hear music. A *pianis-simo* version of *Autumn in New York.* Someone in that dark old house had talent, though the instrument needed tuning.

As I started up the porch stairs I saw a woman sitting at an upright. She appeared nude in the mellow glow that flickered from a lantern wick, the sole light in the room.

When our eyes met, it didn't change her playing, and she didn't let on in any way that I was crossing the porch. She just watched me and played.

I felt a pressure begin at my temples, got my Colt in my hand, and stopped.

What was going on here?

Jazz-flavored cocktail piano. Odor of burning kerosene. A voice—

I turned my good ear toward the room and heard a man speaking. I couldn't make out what he was saying over the piano and the raspy static of the insect chorus behind me.

As I moved up to the door, I got a better look at the woman who had appeared naked at first glance—just skin and a full mane of red hair. But she was in fact wearing a red bra and matching panties.

I put an eye around the edge of the doorjamb and was a moment sorting things out. The wavering lantern light threw shadows that softened edges and distorted what I saw.

In among some tables and chairs, my partner Otis was seated facing me, looking a shade formal in his three-piece suit. A heavyset young man in a short sleeve shirt stood in front of him, his back to me.

Just as I peered in, the man punched Otis in the face, a beaten face that said it wasn't the first punch my partner had suffered that evening.

My heart rate picked up.

A tall guy with thinning hair and dark-framed glasses stood on the other side of Otis. He had a .38 Smith & Wesson in his fist and was the solitary reason my partner was taking a beating. Where the tall man stood and the fact that his weapon was pointed at Otis was why I hadn't already killed him.

I didn't see anybody else besides the exhibitionist at the upright, so I pulled my other Colt from beneath my arm, cocked both, and entered.

"Pay attention," I said as I walked toward the three of them, my hands up with arms extended, my pistols aimed at Specs.

2

THE BIG MAN dishing out the punishment whipped his head around and said, "Wha...?" He gave me a hard look and then glanced past me, curious about what happened to Baby Face, was my guess.

Or wondering if I was alone.

Specs brought his revolver to bear on me as soon as I spoke up. I covered the two men and shifted my direction to an angle that kept the redheaded piano player in my peripheral vision.

"Who dies first?" I said, and stopped about a dozen feet away from them. Even a bad shot could kill at that distance, and they both knew it. My hands were steady. They could see that, too.

They looked like twenty-five-year-old insurance salesmen. Or maybe cops. Similar brown shoes, brown slacks, pistol holsters on their belts, short sleeve shirts open at the collars, cigarette packs in their pockets.

Big Man's acne-scarred face must've cost him girlfriends in high school. For sure the broken capillaries in his swollen nose were costing him lady friends now. "Wait a minute..." he began.

"Shut up," I said. "Move back and keep your hands where I can see them."

"You took your time," Otis said to me, then hawked up a mouthful of blood and spit it on Specs' white shirt.

"Damn it," Specs said, making a face and stepping back, but keeping his weapon on me.

Otis knocked his chair over as he got to his feet. The men shifted their positions to accommodate the new arrangement, but as long as Specs and I did our Mexican standoff, what Otis did was secondary.

The bounce and rattle of the chair hitting the floor made me realize that the music hadn't stopped. It was still easy, still pleasing to the ear, still odd that it was happening at all.

"Now, hold on, little girl..." Big Man started again.

He stopped talking as I shifted the aim of both my weapons to his flushed face. I took a lazy step to the side, lined up the two men, and brought one of my pistols back to Specs. They got it. This wasn't my first standoff.

Otis turned away and shuffled toward the back of the room.

"Where you going?" Specs said.

"Fuck you," Otis replied under his breath and approached the bar where the lantern was placed, bathing us in his moving shadow as he eclipsed the light. Without hurrying, he picked up his fedora from the bar top and pinched the creases before putting it on.

"You're making a mistake," Big Man said to me, and I shifted both pistols back to him.

The redhead stopped playing and looked out the door.

I turned.

It was Baby Face coming across the porch with a snub-nose in his hand. Blood stained his face and neck from the gash I'd opened in his head.

I dropped to one knee as he fired at me. My sense of it was the slug went over me, where I would've been if I hadn't ducked down.

What I knew for sure was he missed me.

The shot I put in his shoulder made him lose his pistol, but it didn't stop him. He stumbled forward a couple of steps, finally collapsing to the floor and sliding toward me on his face, fulfilling the rash momentum he'd brought with him through the door.

I turned, my ears ringing from the gunfire, to find Big Man and Specs hunkered down, fearful of Baby Face's indiscriminate aim. Neither had moved to take advantage of the confusion. I came to my feet with both men still covered.

Big Man said, "You didn't have to shoot him."

Otis rose from behind the bar and said, "*He* shot at *her*, you simple turd. He's lucky she didn't plug his eye out."

The sound of Otis cocking the .38 he'd taken from his ankle holster was like a tiny lightning snap in that quiet space. When he leveled the revolver at Specs, I shifted both my pistols to him, as well, and began backing over to the man on the floor.

"You're outgunned now, ain't you?" Otis said.

Big Man sucked his breath in with such force even I heard it. "Shit. Shit," he said.

"Come here," Otis said to Specs. "Come over here and put that piece on the bar or faster'n a hog farts you ain't gonna be nothing but someone's recollection."

"Do what he says, Herbert. Do what he says," Big

Man said, his double chin undulating as he shook his head.

Herbert didn't like the position he was in. The frozen grimace on his face proved it. But before he had to make up his mind, Baby Face groaned and stirred.

I flicked his pistol away with the toe of my boot.

He looked up at me and said, "I fouled myself."

He had, too. The disgusting stench that rose from him threatened to mask the bitter pall of spent gunpowder and burning kerosene that had already enveloped the room.

He tried to sit up. "My shoulder..."

His brains were rattled. His eyelids fluttered. His face sagged and his head dropped to the floor with a thunk. He was out.

"I ain't telling you again," Otis said to Herbert.

"Well, uh, Herbert. Ya see, don'cha?" Big Man sounded sincere.

Herbert squinted behind his fogging glasses, lowered his Smith & Wesson, walked over, and put it on the bar. Otis motioned with his .38, and Herbert took a .45 out of his belt and put that on the bar, too. Otis then changed weapons, ending up with his own .45 in his hand.

Otis told Herbert, "Get over there," and when the man turned away, Otis slugged him in the head with his heavy weapon. That sent the tall man's specs flying as he fell to the floor with a nasty gash behind his ear.

Otis then stepped around the end of the bar and put his heel down hard on the fingers of Herbert's hand. The crushing of bones was easy to hear in the quiet room. Herbert didn't make a sound, but he'd make some when he woke up.

"Oh, my God," Big Man whispered.

Otis pushed his .45 into his shoulder holster and his .38 into his ankle holster.

"Why'd you have to do that?" Big Man said.

"He won't point a rod at me again," Otis said. "In fact, I want him to cross the street if he sees me coming."

"Okay. We gave you some shit, but we didn't break no bones."

"Don't go Sunday school on me," Otis said. "I come here to trade. Pure and simple. You started the rough stuff."

"We was following orders," Big Man said.

"Since you're so good at following orders, sit down," Otis said.

The man glanced at me, picked up the chair my partner had knocked over, and sat down on it.

Otis doubled up his fist as he started toward him.

Another eye-shift to me, and then Big Man's lids closed. "Mmmmmm," he hummed, in anticipation of my partner slugging him.

Otis's punch had enough heat in it to knock the seated man unconscious. It was a downward chopping right jab that caught him high on his jaw. His whole body jerked to the side and then wilted to the floor, his glazed eyes and misshapen face leading the parade.

The chair spun away on one leg, fell over with a clatter, and slid to a stop.

"A bunch of kids," Otis said, and heaved a sigh.

That was that. The filthy tavern floor was littered with—whatever they were.

I stashed my pistols.

Otis took out his handkerchief to blot his bloody gums,

his cheekbone, and the open place at the corner of his mouth. I gathered my spent brass from shooting Baby Face and put it in my pocket.

"You know who gave him his orders?" I asked Otis under my breath.

Otis sighed. "Damnit, I should've found that out before I knocked him silly."

"Mmmm," I said in agreement.

I gathered up Specs' pistol that Otis left on the bar, and the .38 Special from Big Man's holster and tossed them over to bounce and clunk into a dark corner.

After that it was quiet, except for the hiss of the lantern wick cutting the dead air.

The pianist stood up.

She understood timing. She owned the stage and seemed content there in her own melancholy way.

Otis and I watched as she tiptoed over to the bar on bare feet, pinching a highball glass by its lip in one hand and gripping the neck of an almost empty fifth of vodka in the other. She wore her skimpy attire with indifference, not in the least self-conscious.

Late twenties. Firm, if a bit slender. I was taller and heavier. She had a wan beauty with sad green eyes, a little turned-up nose, and a redhead's translucent skin—cheeks and shoulders dusted with pale freckles. Dangling filigreed silver earrings. Pampered hands and feet. Shaved legs and clean, glistening hair the deep red of ripe strawberries.

On the first finger of her right hand she wore a delicate silver ring with a small diamond setting. Until it sparkled, I hadn't noticed it.

The redhead was Travis Horner's girly pet.

I saw the angry tip of an appendectomy scar peeking

out from her underwear. I'm sure Otis noticed it, too. I also saw a folded red dress on a stool at the other end of the bar. He may have missed that and the red sandals on the floor close by.

She splashed a couple of fingers of vodka into her glass and lifted it as she gave my partner a seductive glance. And in a voice accented by the Ozarks and as dreamy as her piano technique, she said, "Wanna share this one, Otis?"

I glanced at my partner. Had I used his name? Did the redhead know him?

Before Otis could respond, a man's voice from behind us said, "You can forget all that. Get your hands in the air."

3

WE'D BEEN TRICKED by a woman in her underwear.

Otis, okay. But me?

The man who'd gotten the drop on us had a calm voice with a muffled quality. "You can turn around, but don't get cute," he said, exhibiting an accent identical to the redhead's.

He was walking at us from wherever he'd been back in the dark room—a thin little guy with a big .45 in his small fist. The wad of chewing tobacco that knobbed out his cheek accounted for the muffled voice. He wore his gray cowboy hat tipped back.

"Up, up," he cautioned Otis, whose hands had fallen a bit.

His faded yellow cowboy-tight cotton shirt was tucked into pale, washed-out blue jeans held up by an alligator belt and a silver buckle almost as big as the one Otis wore.

"Get on your duds, doll," he told the pianist, who knocked back her drink as if it were water.

The cowboy with the big pistol was mid-thirties or, more likely, a hard drinking twenty-eight or -nine. Foxy face. Ozark cheekbones similar to the redhead's. But his tired brown eyes were more deep-set than hers, and he had a two-day growth of stubble.

A languid wiggle helped the redhead get her dress on over her head. And, as Otis eyeballed her, I observed the cowboy. There was something not right. In the movies cowboys wore their hats back like that so the camera could see their faces. In real life, the big brim kept the sun out of your eyes and the rain from running down your neck.

As the redhead's face appeared from the gathered red rayon that whispered over her shoulders, she said, "Don't kill anybody, Lester."

Her plaintive tone implied that killing was what Lester had done the last time, or that was what she wanted us to believe. He didn't look the part, but real killers often didn't. Pretty Boy Floyd came to mind. He was from the Ozarks, too.

"I don't wanna deal no death here," he said. "But I will, you know. I will if they up and fool with me." The vein that angled across his forehead indicated a slow, steady heartbeat. A calm cowboy in a broke-in hat and scuffed-up alligator boots.

He was small, especially in comparison to Otis, who was very big, but still, the cowboy had a .45 in his fist. No argument about size there.

The redhead finished buttoning her dress, and then steadied herself against the bar as she lifted her pedicured feet one at a time to brush her soles clean, slow and easy, a theatrical prelude to slipping on her sandals. She was way too dressed up for that dump.

"What do you want, Lester?" Otis said.

"What I'm gettin'," the cowboy shot back. And then

to me, he said, "You goin' to a funeral dressed like that?"

I'd heard that before because I always wore black.

"I'm ready," the redhead said, and picked up a glittery red clutch bag that had been on the stool beneath her folded dress.

"Bring the jalopy around, doll. I'll finish up here."

Finish up?

Otis saw my nerves go raw and threw me a glance to do nothing.

The redhead gave Otis a look that lingered and touched her fingertips to the bottle of vodka. "I'll leave this for you," she said.

"Scoot over when you get 'er out front. I'll be drivin'," Lester called after the sad pianist as she headed out the back way, and then he wrinkled up his nose, looked around, and said, "Who's stinking up the place?" He bobbed his chin toward poor Baby Face. "Is he dead?"

"No," I said.

"Whoooee, smells like he is." The cowboy showed us his even little tobacco-stained teeth in a lopsided smile opposite the lump in his cheek. He nodded his head at Otis and said again, "Smells like he is."

To me, he said, "Who you supposed to be in that wig? June Allyson?"

I kept quiet. Ivy, my beautician, said I looked like Gloria DeHaven. Uh huh. Not on my best day, but at least the wig hid my platinum blonde hair.

"Makes you look too growed up. You can't be more'n nineteen or twenty."

We heard a car start up.

I should've looked behind the house.

"You two got gumption. I'll give you that." He turned his head and let fly an ocher stream of tobacco juice that splashed to the floor near Baby Face's feet. "You're funny as a circus side show, too."

"How do you figure that?" Otis was growing tired of Lester.

Lester ignored the question, dabbed at his mouth with a stained handkerchief, and spoke to me again. "I say you're a blonde under there judgin' from that fair skin of yours."

When the redhead was out front, she honked and Lester returned his handkerchief to his hip pocket.

"Well, good night, Mister. Good night, June," he said and backed up. He stopped in the doorway and added, "Don't show a face out this here door unless you can catch bullets in your teeth." He raised his eyebrows and nodded at Otis. "Part of your side show act. Get it?" Another lopsided grin and he was gone from sight.

When we heard his boots on the porch steps, Otis started for the bar. As their car pulled away, I stepped over to the door and watched them bounce down the drive.

"What're they in?" Otis asked.

"Hudson," I said. "Red over something dark. Black, I think."

"New?"

"Could be. I don't know Hudsons so well."

"Which way'd they go?"

"Toward town," I said as I walked over to him.

He took a swig from the bottle of vodka, swished it around like mouthwash, and spit it out to the side.

"Stings like the dickens," he said, and set the bottle aside. He glanced at the boys on the floor. "They ain't gonna snooze forever. Let's get their wallets and skedaddle."

Baby Face, Big Man, and Herbert turned out to be moonlighting Oklahoma City uniformed cops doing some tricky business in civilian clothes. But they were cops, so we'd been made. Otis was more made than I was. I'd just been a white female in a wig. The local law…well, to be precise, some dirty young cops knew us.

We put their names to memory before leaving the tavern.

"They'll be looking for us," I said, and tossed their wallets and badges over into the weeds as we walked down the porch steps.

"More'n likely, but there ain't gonna be no official search."

"They'll have to explain a bullet wound and a broken hand," I said.

"Still'n all, they ain't gonna want us telling our side of the story."

"Unless it's bad all the way to the top."

Otis shook his head. "You always have to sniff a thing twice, don't you, Missy? Stand back."

He flattened the Packard's back tire with one shot from his .45. It took two shots to blow open the trunk.

He handed me the little leather bag. "You take the money. If I get stopped, the police might could start poking around, since my face is cut up and all."

We waded through the weeds over to our cars.

"Go in front," he said. "Get a little lead on me. Know your way?"

"To the Skirvin Hotel?"

"Yeah."

"Back to Tenth Street. That to Broadway."

"You got it."

I tossed the moneybag into the car. Over the roof, I said, "Otis…"

"Yeah?"

"Sorry I was late."

"I figured it was the twister. You see the thing?"

"Not really."

"Big news on the radio," he said. I nodded. "It was smart how you handled the kid, Missy. We don't need no killings on our hands."

"Especially boys with badges," I said. "I must've missed something when you told me about this. I thought it was supposed to be a friendly exchange of goods."

"Mmmm." He opened his car door, and pitched in his fedora. "We'll talk after we get this money back where it belongs. You hungry?"

"I could eat."

"And I could use some coffee," he said.

"Sorry you got punched around," I said.

"Don't matter. Takes more'n that."

"You're gonna have a shiner."

He put his fingertips to his eye. "He wouldn't have hurt me at all except for that ring he was wearing. I'm getting soft. Time was, I'd've cut his finger off."

That last was to himself as he lowered his big frame into his car.

I drove out ahead of him.

4

ONCE ON THE deserted highway, I did some think-ing.

The reason for a backup when you're doing a trade is simple. Without someone riding shotgun, when you show up, they can kill you and take the money. That's the part about bagmen not getting respect.

But what happened at Curly's Tavern didn't make sense. Who was going to win out of that mess? The girl-friend took off with a cowboy named Lester with no money being involved at all. At least we were able to corral the cash. How stupid would it have been if we had lost the redhead *and* ended up without the ransom money?

Travis Horner had a passel of ex-wives. I didn't know if he was married at the moment or not and, to be candid, I didn't really care what happened to the womanizer or his redheaded mistress. In the time I'd been doing PI work with Otis, I'd seen enough infidelity to last a lifetime. But like it or not, she was half of the job—pay the money, bring the girlfriend home.

Moonlighting amateur cops, though. What part of the

job were they? Who could have predicted those trigger-happy imbeciles?

And who the hell was Lester?

I was looking forward to some answers. However, I probably wasn't going to get them from Otis. He didn't act as if he knew much more than I did, except there was that strange business between him and the redhead. Did they know each other?

Out of the darkness, lightning pinballed across the heavens in a fiery display. After a few moments, thunder crackled in the distance. It was going to rain some more and it wasn't that far away.

I saw something in that burst of brightness.

Far ahead a car stopped on the shoulder.

I switched on my high beams, illuminating two figures in an area beside the road. My first thoughts were of Lester and the redhead.

The figures were tiny at that distance. But I could see they were—what were they doing? Struggling. One was trying to get away from the other.

I was drawing closer.

It was a tall, lanky man and a woman.

That man was not little Lester.

The woman pulled free, stumbled back, and fell. He grabbed at her and dragged her a step or two, but she fought him. He looked at my approaching headlights, hesitated, and then hurried away through the thick grass like a high-stepping stork.

The waiting car began moving while the tall guy was still getting into the passenger side. They sped away, but not before I saw that it was a Pontiac with Texas plates.

As I approached the area where the Pontiac had been, I saw lights back in the trees. Another car.

The Hudson.

Lester's car had left the road and plowed into a thick stand of scrub oaks. That made the woman the redheaded pianist, didn't it?

I pulled over and jumped out, leaving my engine running and my lights on.

A fenceless, wide apron of tall grass separated the narrow shoulder of the road from the edge of the woods. My headlights were enough to guide me to where the woman in the red dress lay in the wet grass, crying.

"You're safe now," I said when I knelt down beside her. "Are you hurt? Did they hurt you?" She cried harder, so I held and comforted her until Otis drove up.

He hustled over to us. "We get our girl after all," he said, catching his breath.

He gathered her to him and stood up with her in his arms. She clung to his neck, sobbing, snuggling her blood-splattered, tear-streaked face against his shoulder like she'd been there before. She was accustomed to protection—childlike.

Otis and I looked over to where the Hudson idled. The exhaust hung heavy in the soggy woods, creating a glowing red haze around the taillights. All the car's lights were on, including the interior lights, and through the colored vapor we could make out the driver's door standing open.

"What've we got here?" Otis asked.

I picked up a sandal that the pianist had lost as I told him about seeing the distant struggle, the tall man strutting through the grass, the car pulling away.

"Texas tags?"

I nodded. "What do you make of that?"

He glanced toward the road. "Not sure I know, but

it ain't smart to hang around chawin'." The sky lit up, bathing us in cold light.

I slipped the sandal into his coat pocket, and said, "I'll take a look."

"Missy…"

"I know," I said, and walked off as the thunder rattled in the distance.

Violent things happen to people who carry guns, and the car that pulled away had not borne Good Samaritans. I felt certain that the occupants of that vehicle were involved in whatever mischief had sent the Hudson careening off the road and caused blood splatter on the redhead's face.

I pulled my pistol, watched ahead of me, and listened, but the only sound, besides the incessant chirp of insects and the swishing cadence of my progress through the moist grass, was the low rumble of the Hudson's powerful engine.

The heavy car had gouged tracks in the soft soil and flattened a swath of grass as it left the highway and raced headlong into the dark woods. Following those tracks into the crimson exhaust was like moving through Satan's breath.

The trunk lid was up. Empty. Had they found what they were looking for? By the open driver's door, I discovered the little cowboy, draped half out of the car, face down in the dirt, his big pistol and old hat near him, his pastel shirt discolored by his blood.

Lester had taken a hit or two while driving, from the looks of the broken side window and bloody car interior, and a few more point-blank into his back after the door was pulled open and he fell out. Was the shooter taking no chances, or just vicious?

I coughed. My throat was getting rough even though I was holding my breath as much as I could. I holstered my weapon, straddled the little guy's legs, leaned into the air-conditioned space, and shut off the idling engine. I found the red clutch bag on the seat, stuffed it into my jacket pocket, and switched off all the lights.

The discovery of that murder was going to be best left to some innocent passerby that held no concern about being named in the morning papers. I put the steam on getting back to my car.

I was driving down the highway a good distance before I saw Otis pull out behind me, and it wasn't long after that I lost sight of his headlights altogether. I was going to get to the city ahead of them because I was driving and they were talking.

I was far ahead of Otis and the redhead when the Pontiac two-door came at me with its high beams glaring and whizzed by like a cat with its tail on fire. It was the guys who'd shot up the cowboy.

The driver looked over as they passed. A face only a mother could love.

Brake lights.

To the rearview mirror, I said, "You think she's with me, don't you, Ugly."

Okay. I cranked my buggy up to eighty, hugged the middle of the asphalt, and prayed for no wildlife to wander onto the road as the rural nightscape streamed by.

I rehashed the last few plays.

They murdered Lester and tried to snatch the redhead.

I scared them off and they decided to come back.

Something changed their minds. What?

Maybe they needed time to mull it over before returning

to the scene of the crime. Maybe a lot of stuff, but one thing was obvious. The boy cops. The little cowboy. The killers behind me in the Pontiac. My partner and I. Everybody wanted the redhead.

I was, at that moment, leading Ugly and his lanky passenger on a chase that would take them away from Otis and his redheaded passenger. That was easy, but it was also loose. My partner didn't know what was happening, plus things could get weird.

Or, considering the evening as a whole, things could get weirder.

What to do?

Hell, I had questions and who better to ask than those two?

Far ahead I could see that the road cut through a wooded area. Trees crowded the highway on both sides. I brought my speed down in a hurry, pulled onto the shoulder, and killed the engine. I jumped out, leaving the lights on.

I knew what I wanted and where it was. I was in and out of the trunk in a jiffy.

With an eye out for lights in the distance, I ran across the road, broke through the underbrush and into the trees on the other side. On that dark night in my black clothes and dark wig I would be lost to the naked eye.

I paused by one of the bigger trees at the edge of the dank woods and waited. Driving fast had given me a good lead. The silence was eerie until the whine of mosquitoes, and then the rest of the night creatures started again.

It was never quiet in the woods at night.

5

LIGHTS APPEARED IN the distance. They came up and over a small rise and rushed at me from the darkness, silent and surreal, finally cutting their speed as they grew near. Then, the Pontiac pulled off the highway and rolled up behind my car with its lights out. Cops called that maneuver a blackout. But those two goons were not the law. They were murderers who thought the redhead was in my car.

They sat there for a moment, engine idling. Ugly, the driver, had his elbow stuck out the window. He glanced my direction once, but not right at me. Their attention was on my car.

When the passenger door opened, the interior lights came on, and before Ugly switched them off, I saw that the two of them were alone. The driver was a jowly guy with big shoulders, mostly bald; the gray hair above his ears was cut short.

Thin Man had a long handsome face in profile. Gary Cooper came to mind. I also saw the flash of a revolver in his hand. A serious piece; a .44 maybe. He was all angles, younger than Ugly, and he unfolded from the car with a liquid motion that comes from strength.

I waited until he had glanced over the roof, checked all directions, and stepped around his door before I started out of the trees.

I was counting on the Pontiac's idling engine to cover the sound of me crossing the road. I wanted to take control of the situation before Thin Man discovered my car was empty. I approached the Pontiac from behind, bent over and staying at an angle that kept me out of the driver's side mirror.

Thin Man was making his way toward my car, keeping his eyes to the front. I was out of his view if he should look my way.

The grumbling of the big V8 was the solitary sound.

I could feel the heat and smell the engine as I brought up the short-barreled, pistol grip 12-gauge that I had taken from my trunk.

When I jammed the shotgun through the open window and hard into the driver's bull neck, his backbone stiffened and he gripped the wheel with both hands.

"Easy," I whispered along the barrel and into his ear.

For a moment, neither of us moved as we watched his pal sneaking up on the right rear corner of my car.

I pressed the shotgun tight against his neck and whispered, "Leave your left on the wheel, and take your piece out with two fingers."

I watched Thin Man making his way along the right side of my car as Ugly moved in exaggerated slow motion to remove a Smith .357 from beneath his arm. Those boys liked heavy weapons.

"Throw it over your shoulder into the backseat. Gently. Gently," I whispered.

He did that, but, as he pitched the pistol, he revved the engine.

Damn it.

Thin Man's head snapped our direction.

Ugly made his move, coming across his face fast with the hand that had tossed the pistol. He pushed the shotgun up.

I put a load of double ought buck through the roof of the car, an earsplitting discharge that sent a sharp pain through my head, and no doubt deafened Ugly. He yanked the steering wheel to the right and pulled the gearshift as he dropped down across the seat.

It was happening fast.

The car was in reverse and turning into me as the front end whipped out onto the roadway.

I'd held the gun in both hands and staggered back from the recoil, but I didn't retreat fast enough to keep from being brushed hard by the moving front fender.

I stumbled a step or two with my legs tangled before hitting the rough pavement on my backside. That hurt like hell, because I still had my blackjack in my hip pocket.

My ears were ringing, but I still heard the engine winding up.

I rolled over and came up facing the Pontiac. It was crashing back into the trees, tires whining. Ugly was out of sight, still down in the seat with the gas pedal to the metal.

I chambered a fresh shell and searched the woods for Thin Man before taking out the front window of the car to keep Ugly down. The recoil from that second shot damn near tore the gun from my grip.

I scrambled to my feet and racked in another shell as I backpedaled across the road, looking everywhere for the shooter.

I was on the other side when the car's headlights came on. I wasn't in the direct light, but the spill got me. My heart was seriously trying to break a rib as I tore through the sodden underbrush. I was ten feet into the woods before I slid to the ground and scrambled around, ending up flat on my stomach behind a good-sized tree trunk. I wasn't out of breath, but I was breathing hard.

I saw him across the road. Coming out of the trees, high stepping through the underbrush, mostly shadow. He was close to the car, charging for the open passenger door. I led him and fired low at the last moment, just above the flat asphalt road, clipping the bottom of the front fender, aiming beneath the open car door.

I hit the car door and him, too. Or, at least I thought I hit him.

He looked at me before his face disappeared behind the car door.

He was smiling.

And then I was taking fire.

Christ!

I stretched back to get as much of me behind the tree as I could. Thunderous cracks from Ugly's cannon echoed through the woods, alarming birds to flight. The driver was shooting at me from the car, and he knew where I was.

Another pistol joined in. Those men were blasting large caliber slugs at me. My heart was racing. I didn't like the awful *kathunk kathunk* of lead slamming into my oak tree and tearing out chunks of the trunk and barreling into the ground around me. I liked even less the *swishing* of heated lead passing my head.

I kept my shoulders scrunched up to stay narrow as I squirmed to get a .38 in each hand. I returned fire from both sides of my tree trunk, blindly snapping off shot after shot. It sounded like a firing range. My hearing went flat from the noise. But the racket didn't last long. They were out of bullets by the time I got started.

The moment their shooting stopped, their car was throwing gravel.

I looked out from my cover and saw the smoking tires peeling rubber as they bounced up onto the asphalt, and roared away. A hubcap broke loose and rolled after the fleeing Pontiac, finally clattering to a stop somewhere out there in the darkness.

When my heart settled down, I exhaled, got to my feet, and gave myself a hard-earned compliment: "That plan was well thought out."

6

I WAS EMERGING from the woods brushing away dirt and leaves when the Buick drove up. The stench of gunfire and burning rubber still hung in the air.

As Otis got out, putting on his hat, he gave me one of those what-have-you-done-now looks as we met in his headlights.

He eyed the shotgun I carried by my leg, out of sight from his passenger. "What gives?"

I glanced over at the redhead. Her expression was so—open. She seemed as innocent as a child. A child with blood on her face.

"The guys who killed Lester thought I had her. We were just going to talk about it when the shooting started."

"Uh huh," Otis said, and then spoke across the hood. "Turn out the lights, will you, Savannah?"

"That's her name?"

"Yep. It's where her granny was born. Good thing she weren't born in Tuscaloosa."

The Buick's headlights went off.

He pulled out a Lucky and fired up as he followed me to the trunk of my car. I kept my back to Savannah and reloaded the cut-off shotgun before putting it away. While I was doing that, I told Otis what I'd done and why and how it had gone south.

"Next time let me worry about me. You just high-tail it."

"You can count on it," I said.

"How'd you call 'em?"

"Thin Man and Ugly. The tall guy looks like a scrawny Gary Cooper. Ugly is a bulldog. Ring any bells?"

"I'm not getting anything."

"I think I got the lanky guy's ankle or foot."

"Yeah?"

"The strange thing is, he grinned like a fool."

"He smiled when you shot him?"

"Odd, huh?"

"A full-blood Crow I know does that. The more you hurt 'im, the more he smiles. Some guys ain't dead till you kill 'em."

I noticed something like a burning sensation. I felt around and discovered some genuine pain in my right arm near the shoulder along with a small tear in my jacket. I found a second tear in the leather where the bullet had come out. The area between was growing more sensitive to my touch. Adrenaline must've masked the pain until then.

Otis said, "Let's see, Missy," and helped me take off my jacket.

"I just bought this."

"That's what you're worried about, is it?"

I held the coat over my arm. "It wasn't cheap."

"Uh huh, and it looks swell on you, too. Gimme a knife."

I moved so he blocked the redhead's line of sight,

slipped a knife from my boot and gave it to him pommel first.

"Careful," I said.

"Sharp as a straight razor, ain't it?"

"Sharper," I told him, and turned so he had better light from the trunk before he sliced my shirt between the holes.

He pulled open the fabric and looked at the place. "It ain't much. Just grazed you. Bet it smarts, though."

I craned my neck and looked at the dark groove. "It's like a burn. No blood."

"Cauterized itself, I reckon. Good as a miss."

"It hurts a lot for a miss."

"It ain't like you to act like a sissy," he said. "A little more to the inside and it would've took bone. Different kettle of fish. We'll patch you up when we get someplace clean to do it."

I retrieved my blade and put it away.

"Did she talk to you?" I asked.

He glanced back. Savannah was watching, but was too far away to hear us.

"She talked," he said, as he helped me get on a black Levi's jacket I took from the trunk. "She's a peculiar girl. That's her brother they killed back there."

"How's she taking it?"

"She cried hard and then seemed to forget about it. She just wants to snuggle."

"Snuggle?"

"You know, get up close."

"What's going on, Otis?"

"Let's get her back where she belongs and see if we can find out. Nobody said nothin' about killers and dirty cops, and I ain't liking any part of it."

As he stepped away, he noticed a streak of dampness on the asphalt and bent down to check it out. It ran up the road where the Pontiac had gone.

"You shoot their radiator?"

"I was firing from behind a tree. I don't know what I hit."

Otis eyed the distance. "They're gonna be up the road with a motor hotter'n summer in Odessa." He walked toward his car. "I'll go first, you tuck in behind with your lights out. We'll go by before they can say Jack Robinson."

As predicted, the Pontiac was beside the road with the hood up and smoke pouring out. I didn't see the thugs as we sped by, but they were there somewhere, and I had to wonder what would happen next for them.

If I'd hit the thin man like I thought, he wouldn't be walking anywhere; that left hitching a ride to the nearest station, arranging for the car, and getting medical attention. It was the middle of the night, and I hadn't seen any traffic out on that road. My guess was they were in for a long, unpleasant night.

So what?

The more difficult life was for them, the better I liked it.

But the real question was, why were they out there in the first place?

When we stopped at a filling station so Savannah could clean the blood splatter from her face, Otis and I had another chance to talk.

"I was thinking about the guys in the Pontiac," I said.

"Yeah?"

"They're pros, Otis, up from Texas, so we know who they're working for."

"Horner ain't the only man who lives in Texas, but I get your drift."

"They knew where to find the girl."

"I said I get it." I knew the look. I waited. "I met this Savannah once."

"Yeah. I got that."

I waited again.

Finally, he said, "When Travis called, he told me her name and that he wanted me to bring her back to him. I had to be reminded who she was. It was ten years or so ago."

"Ten years? She couldn't've been more than seventeen or eighteen."

"Yeah. That's about right, just a young thing. She was on the wrong side of Dallas, out where she shouldn't've been. Just dumb luck I even saw her, but I did. Some men had her in their car."

He remembered for a moment.

"I put a stop to that."

He had never taken kindly to men who abuse women. Otis when he was forty. My god, whatever he did to them, it was bad.

He took a breath.

"I got her cleaned up and onto a bus to Oklahoma. It was back when I was drinking. Lucky it happened when it did. An hour later…"

"Did you tell Horner about that?"

He shook his head. "She must've told 'im. No one knew but us two."

"Why'd he call you?"

"He said she'd trust me; she'd go with me."

"But if you were there to buy her back, why wouldn't she go with you no matter who you were?"

"He said she could be talked into things. He wasn't sure what she might say or do."

"Travis Horner was a friend of yours?"

"We wasn't really friends, just hung around at some of the same joints. When you're drinking, there's no telling who you'll take up with."

"That clears up part of it, but there's still what happened tonight. Those thugs on the highway were after Savannah, that's plain. But what else were they up to?"

"Wha'd'you mean, Missy?"

"I think those boys were off their plan. If they came up from Texas, they probably got delayed by the same tornado that slowed me down."

"Yeah?"

I said, "They were on their way to that old tavern, weren't they? But they were late. They saw Savannah and Lester and you know the rest of it. If they'd shown up while she was still at the tavern…"

"Maybe them boy cops was just delayin' things by messin' around with me."

"Who knows? But the shooters were off their plan. I think that's for sure."

"Otherwise, you're sayin' Savannah'd be with them right now and we'd be dead as doornails in that old tavern?"

"Along with the boy detectives," I said.

Otis stared at me for a long moment. "That's how you see it?"

"Those boys are shooters, not negotiators. They wanted the girl. The rest of us were fodder."

7

THE NIGHT LIT up and Otis and I gazed up at the sky until it was over. In the distance there was the deep shuffle of thunder. Otherwise, it was quiet, save for some music playing.

The filling station was deserted except for our cars and the Chevy convertible that belonged to the kid on night shift. After he cleaned the bugs off our windshields, he hadn't given us another thought; his girlfriend was there and they were sitting in the ragtop making eyes and listening to Ray Charles.

Finally, my partner heaved a sigh and said, "All the evidence is there, but I don't get it." He gave his head a shake like he was waking up. "He gets me into this with hogwash about how she'll go with me, but sends some shooters to knock me off. How does he gain from that?"

"He ends up with the redhead and you dead. That's all I see."

"Well, yeah…" Otis said, giving me a sidelong glance.

"And no idea why, huh?"

"Not a clue, Missy."

"Try this. He needed a patsy for some play he has going down; he thought of you and used the girl to get you out where his boys could take you out."

"Well, you trumped that move, didn't you, Missy? Sticking your nose in like you always do...like everything's your beeswax."

Otis was sounding like himself again.

"I ain't been thinking clear," he said. "Thinking about that Savannah girl all them years ago instead of the job."

"Maybe that's what he was counting on."

He gave me a long look and I waited.

"Well, Missy. The first thing we do is give them boys out by the road something to keep them busy. We don't want no more of their shit tonight."

I followed his giant strides to the payphone and provided some change so he could call the police. He told the law they should go out and investigate an accident, and gave them directions.

"You better watch out, too," he added. "There's been some shooting. Them guys with the Pontiac are armed and dangerous."

When we saw Savannah coming from the restroom, Otis winked at me and said, "Let's go straighten out a few things with Mister Travis Horner."

I'm not a gambler. Well, I don't gamble on most things, but I'd bet Otis' ex-wife Dixie figured into this thing between my partner and Horner. Back in those days she always seemed to be testing Otis one way or another.

I never pushed Otis about his life before I met him that

winter of '53, but I knew he'd had some rough years, full of deceit, drinking, and mayhem. Every now and again he would say something about Dixie. No details really. But what I did hear made his past seem like a half-put-together jigsaw puzzle.

I knew one thing, though. Dixie had broken his heart and he still hadn't put it back together.

8

IT WAS SPRINKLING rain by the time we got to downtown Oklahoma City and the Skirvin Hotel. The rain combined with the hour had taken the starch out of the parking lot attendant.

"Anywhere over there," he called out from his dry booth.

When I got out of my car, Otis motioned for me to leave the bag of money.

"We won't be giving that back," he said. "Expenses."

I left my purse, as well. I had what I needed, a .38 under my arm and a .32 at my ankle. The simple exchange of goods that had gotten complicated was simple again.

The pianist and I trotted along beside Otis, hurrying to get out of the light mist.

"They have a tunnel over to where we're going," Otis said, shaking the moisture from his fedora as we entered the hotel.

"A tunnel?" Savannah said.

"That's right," he said.

"I've never been in a tunnel," she said.

As we found our way down the stairs to the concourse that led to the Skirvin Towers across the street, I told Otis, "I found a brochure about this hotel in the glove compartment of my dad's car."

"That Cadillac you used to drive?"

"Uh huh. He and Mom had their honeymoon here."

"Hard to find a nicer hotel in these parts," Otis said. "Me and Dixie stayed here once, too."

That was how he mentioned his ex.

I waited for him to add something. When he didn't, I said, "Yeah?"

"Yeah," he said, and stopped walking. So we all paused there in the concourse.

Otis had something to say, and in a tunnel under Broadway seemed like a private enough place. He spoke in a quiet voice.

"Look, Missy. Savannah told me on the way here that she ran off from Horner. He ain't been nice to her, and there's no way in hell she wants to go back to him. So, we are definitely not leaving her at this hotel."

"Okay," I said, and glanced at Savannah who wouldn't look me in the eye.

Otis put his arm around her shoulders. "She's under our protection, I guess you'd say, until we can get her home."

"And we're here because…?"

"To straighten things out with Horner about all that's happened tonight, then we're on our way."

Over at the Towers, it was as still as a graveyard in the lobby. Savannah and I stopped near a gathering of richly upholstered furniture below a crystal chandelier, while Otis went over to the front desk.

I saw the clerk look up from some paperwork and discover my partner. Otis weighed two-eighty plus and stood six-five plus in his boots. His broken nose and no-nonsense glare said cop or Marine veteran, or pro wrestler or something dangerous. And even if he was fifty, no one in his right mind wanted to mess with him. Add to that the damage Big Man's class ring had done to his face earlier in the evening and the clerk's startled reaction explained itself.

The solitary uniformed bellman noticed us, too. Well, not us. The redhead, shivering in her damp, thin, red dress.

"They keep it chilly in here," I said to her. "You okay?"

"It feels refreshing," she said in that slow drawl of hers, preoccupied with the sly glances she was exchanging with the middle-aged bellhop.

Over the death of her brother so quickly? What was it about her? She acted young. Yet, that wasn't it. Innocent came to mind again, but she wasn't acting innocent. Nor had she been concerned about being in her underwear in front of the men at Curly's Tavern. And, come to think of it, I didn't recall any reaction to the shooting and fighting at the tavern, either. What was her game?

Otis gave me a nod as he walked by, and we followed him.

The bellhop's eyes followed us.

In the elevator car, a uniformed young man with a sleepy face toed a switch that shut the outside doors, and pushed closed a latticed gate. "Floor please," he said.

"Twelve," Otis said.

On the way up, Otis used a calming voice when he spoke to Savannah, like an uncle might. "Almost over with," he said. She smiled at him with a vacant expression and gripped his arm more tightly. I finally got it.

Savannah was what my mother would have called a simple child. That was what Otis had meant when he said she was a peculiar girl.

If I'd spent more time with her, I would have caught it earlier. She wasn't a Loony Tune by any stretch; she just wasn't quite there. She clearly knew how to conduct herself in public, how to dress herself, or maybe I meant undress. But regardless of her looks and her real age, in some significant ways Savannah hadn't fully grown up.

"Have you been here before?" I asked her.

"Where?"

"In this hotel. Have you been here before?"

"I don't think so," she said, and offered me a sweet smile. "It's nice, isn't it?"

Neo-Georgian, the brochure had called the architecture.

Savannah was a puppy on a string; she'd go wherever we took her, and probably for no other reason than we'd been nice to her.

Otis and I exchanged a glance.

"Did you know this?" I asked him, nodding my head at her.

My lack of circumspection caused Otis some discomfort. He wrinkled his face and glanced first at the elevator operator who had been trained to not listen, and then down at our woman/child, but she was taking no notice of us. Her concentration was on the floor numbers lighting up in sequence.

Otis shook his head no.

A soft bell noted our arrival at twelve. The operator

drew back the gate and pulled down the chrome bar that opened the outer door.

As we stepped into the wide hallway, my mind went to the young cops. They had been in over their heads. Hell, they couldn't handle *us*, and we'd meant them no harm. What if they had run up against the boys I'd met on the road?

It had definitely been a setup. Grab the girl and leave everyone dead. And the *everyone* part had been carefully chosen. Rookie cops and a compassionate P.I.

We started down the quiet corridor. Behind us, the elevator doors closed with a faint thunk, and a chill went up my back.

"I have a bad feeling," I said under my breath, and put on my black horn-rimmed clear eyeglasses. I hadn't taken off my brunette wig, so I was ready.

"You ain't going in, Missy."

"No?"

"Keep her safe and watch our backs. You know the drill."

We came to 1210 and Otis knocked.

I placed Savannah behind me and stood where I could see in. I could feel her shuffling about trying to peer around me.

After a moment, a short, dark-haired young guy in a suit and tie opened the door. He kept his handsome face impassive and said nothing. I noticed his shoulder holster, though I knew by the dapper cut of his expensive suit that I wasn't supposed to.

That was all I had time to see before Otis punched him in the jaw. The man disappeared from my view, the door crashed back, and my partner started across the large room.

He'd said not to enter. I knew better. There was always something to clean up. I stepped into the doorway and glanced around the suite checking for additional humanity.

Finding no one extra, my attention went to the dapper doorman with the bloody mouth; he was clearing his head. Next he would be trying to rise.

There was time to glance over to where Otis was going.

Horner was without a tie, in his shirt and suspenders, a little older than I remembered him, graying temples, late forties, thin mustache. He was throwing down his napkin and moving around the table where he'd been eating supper.

The doorman had struggled to his knees by then, so I backhanded him hard with my blackjack, high on his neck across his trapezius muscle, an inducement to stay put.

I looked back at Horner as he said, "Otis! What's going on here?" and lifted his arms like he was welcoming the congregation to come forward.

Otis went forward all right, and socked Travis Horner square in the face.

The force of the blow knocked the good-looking man out of his bedroom slippers, back over his supper table, and onto the floor along with dishes, food, linen, cutlery, and a sparkling cut-crystal vase of white jonquils.

Adding insult to injury, or perhaps, injury to injury, since it was so heavy, Otis tipped the table over on the bootlegger. Then, he stomped the bare ankle that was sticking out on our side. The cry the injured man emitted was miserable enough to almost make me feel sorry for him, but not quite.

Out of the corner of my eye I saw the young doorman pulling himself up again. He had his shoulder raised and held his head to the side, obviously in pain.

"For crying out loud, Dapper Dan," I said. "Stay down," and gave him a blackjack to the head, which opened a nasty gash behind his ear.

All we needed was for that attractive young guy to get frisky enough to pull a piece and start shooting.

The shoulder seam of his blood-splattered suit coat ripped open as I pulled the unconscious lug over onto his back to relieve him of his pistol, a smallish make I wasn't familiar with. I stuffed his peashooter and my blackjack into my back pockets.

All the strain had my injured arm hurting, but I thought I wouldn't whine. There was nothing to be gained from it.

Savannah's open stare met me when I stood up. She'd wandered over to the sideboard and poured herself some vodka.

I motioned for her to come on and started for the door. I had to shift the little pistol to my belt; it wasn't comfortable in my hip pocket, since getting bruised on my backside earlier in the evening.

"Finish your drink, dear," I told the redhead who was staring at the shifting debris under which Travis Horner was struggling to extricate himself.

Keeping her eyes on Horner, she knocked back her vodka and handed me the empty tumbler.

My partner offered up a concerned expression as he strolled over, and said, "They have a doctor on call, don't you imagine? A place like this?"

"Now, Otis. Don't go all mushy on me," I said as I put the redhead's tumbler on a side table.

He gave me a wink as we entered the quiet hall and I closed the door behind us.

Walking toward the elevators, I noticed tears in Savannah's eyes, but a moment later she seemed happy enough when she got to push the down button.

9

"WHAT'S THAT ABOUT?" Otis asked.

I was reading by the glow from the open glove box.

I closed the compartment door and my book, sat back, and gazed out at the damp night flying by. Our headlights were giving us prolonged moments of rain-darkened rail fencing and the murky shapes of farm buildings and narrow roads of shiny mud that angled off into gloomy woodlands.

My car was parked in the lot at the Skirvin. Otis had wrangled a monthly rate from the attendant. He wanted me to join him and Savannah for the drive down to her parents' home in the southeast corner of the state. I looked at her curled up in the backseat and wished I could do that. But reading was more relaxing for me than sleep right then. And, to be honest, it helped keep me from thinking of Lee.

"The book is about...well, it takes place during the Spanish civil war," I told Otis. "Some guerillas need to destroy a bridge. So there's adventure and it's a love story, too. But I guess most of all it's about brotherhood."

"I've seen that book around. You've read it before."

"Uh huh. I like it."

It was quiet in the car. The steady downpour and windshield wipers were making the only sounds. Looking past Otis to the east, the sky was growing light, but the dark clouds were not going away. It was going to be another wet, overcast day.

I was dog-tired.

When I finally did close my eyes, it would be the sleep of the damned.

When we pulled in for gas and a pee break in Antlers, Savannah said she wanted to call her daddy.

"It's five in the morning," I said.

"He's up," she said, and held her hand out for money for the phone.

When we all met back in the car, shaking water off like dogs from a bath, she said, "Daddy'll meet us in Broken Bow. He says we ought not drive in the woods. The back roads turn slippery as all get out when it storms like this."

Savannah was wide-awake and talkative. She had remembered to ask her father to bring her a light sweater, a suggestion that I'd made. We were in rural Oklahoma. I had an idea he wouldn't like seeing his daughter in a dress with the front cut so low.

"I'm so mad I could spit it had to rain today," she said. "It's so nice back in the woods and now you don't get to see it."

"Does your daddy have a farm?" I said.

"My daddy doesn't farm, but my uncle and his hands tend Daddy's trees."

"Your family grows trees?"

"Everybody does that. It's trees everywhere around here." She pointed out the window at the forest we were driving through. "I used to get a nickel for the trees I could name. Oak and hickory and red cedar and cypress and ash and maple and elm and cottonwood and sycamore and beech and hackberry and loblolly pine and yellow poplar. Wanna guess what my favorite tree is?"

"You've already named more trees than I know."

She smiled with pride. "The black tupelo. It's beautiful in the autumn. We have them in our yard. And I like the box elders down by the creek, too. Daddy says they're worthless, but I like their flutter wings." She twirled her finger.

"If your daddy doesn't farm, what kind of work does he do?"

"My daddy's a bootlegger," she said, staring out the window. "My granddaddy was a bootlegger, too."

I saw Otis cut his eyes to the rearview mirror.

"There's a sweet gum," our tree-savvy redhead said, pressing her finger against the rain-streaked glass.

"Did your daddy say where he was going to meet us?"

Savannah nodded and said, "Ida's."

A while back, I'd spent a few years on the road in Texas, hustling pool from one parlor to another, so I'd eaten in a lot of small town cafés. It didn't take long before I knew a good one by just walking in the door.

Ida's Café qualified.

A stone and log construction with a big front porch, it was set back in among tall pines. Pickup trucks dominated the close parking spots, which was too bad for us because the rain had picked up. We almost drowned running from the car.

When we reached the porch, we shook water off and cleaned the mud from our shoes under the sad-eyed scrutiny of two Bluetick coonhounds that were curled up near the door. A long pine plank with big nail heads protruding was fixed to the wall and served as the clothing rack. It was almost filled with coats, jackets, and wet hats.

We could hear the hubbub coming from behind the fogged windows.

The café was last remodeled in the late forties, but the place wasn't about décor. It was about good food. That's why it was so busy. The blended aromas of ham, sausage, bacon, onions, and potatoes and, maybe best of all, fresh coffee welcomed us as we entered the warm room.

The twenty or so husky woodsmen and robust farmers that filled almost every table in the large open space stopped eating their biscuits and gravy and stared at us. I saw the cook and his helper peer out from the kitchen to learn why the place had gone silent. For a long minute, the only sound was the rain pounding on the roof.

It could have been Otis in his three-piece suit and fedora or me in all black with my pale skin and platinum blonde hair, but it wasn't either of us. It was Savannah that hushed the house.

Finally, a prune of a woman wearing wire frame glasses and a beige waitress uniform that hung straight down from her bony shoulders, stepped around the counter and walked slowly toward us in her white, thick-soled shoes. "Is that you, Savannah Smike?" she said.

"Yes, ma'am," Savannah said.

"I thought it was you with that pretty face and that

beautiful hair. Lord love a duck, it's been a spell. You remember me?"

Savannah nodded yes.

"Of course, you do. It's Miss Ida. I taught you Sunday school, but my hair was darker then." Ida smiled and patted her thinning white hair. "You recollect?"

Savannah's face lit up. "I do recollect, Miss Ida."

Ida made a sound that was more cackle than laugh, and said, "Why, you sweet thing. You hug my neck."

"I'm soaking wet, Miss Ida."

"Never you mind. Come on now."

Savannah took a hesitant step forward, Ida filled in the rest of the distance, and they gave each other a hug. No customer moved, not a single facial expression changed as all ears remained on alert and all eyes followed the little drama.

Ida held Savannah at arm's length. "Laws, you always was the sweetest girl. We heard you was playing your music at a fancy place in Dallas."

"I was doing that," Savannah said, her green eyes sparkling.

"Uh huh, we heard you was. You home for a visit?"

"Yes, ma'am."

"On your way to see your daddy?"

Savannah shook her head no, and I saw several in the rapt audience unconsciously imitate her headshake.

"No?"

"The roads are too muddy."

"I see."

Savannah smiled big. "He's coming here, Miss Ida."

Ida exhaled in a rush and under her breath said, "Well, I swan." She glanced around her café. "Bull Smike is on his way here."

As one, the burly lumberjacks and stout farmers rose from their chairs and threw money on the tables. Otis and I moved aside, and in less time than it would take to tell it, Ida's customers streamed out the door, gathered up their coats and hats from the rack on the porch, waded into the downpour to their trucks, and were gone.

"Holy shit," Otis whispered.

Retaining the sweet voice she used for Savannah, Ida said, "I haven't seen your daddy in a coon's age." She paused and cocked her head, perhaps considering if she should discuss something, and then went on. "I wonder if your dear mama'll be with him."

"I don't rightly know, ma'am," Savannah allowed.

"Uh huh. Now, precious, you have to help out like you used to. We need to clear all these tables." And to Otis and me, she said, "Why don't you sit over there and I'll bring you some coffee."

10

OTIS WAS IN the restroom and I was nursing my second cup of java when the door opened.

A tall man wearing a wide-brimmed hat entered. His rain gear was an Army surplus poncho. He looked like any one of the farmers or lumberjacks that had so recently hurried out of Ida's except he carried a pump action Remington 12-gauge and dripped water and tracked mud. I guessed his age at mid-twenties.

He gave the empty room a quick glance and then let his somber gaze settle on me long enough to instill some caution. His attention shifted to Savannah when she came from the kitchen.

"Hello, Eustace," she said to her younger brother.

She was wearing a long white apron she'd put on to protect her dress.

"Savannah," he said.

The door opened behind him and another tall man entered. He, too, carried a 12-gauge and tracked mud in with him. Water dripped from the brim of his felt hat. He wore a shiny black raincoat.

"Hello, Buford," Savannah said from where she'd

stopped in the middle of the room among the tables and chairs.

Buford was the older brother. He remained silent and gave me a long stare. I didn't look away. Why should I? But my mouth went dry. Buford was trouble looking for someplace to happen.

Eustace and Savannah bore a strong resemblance to one another: high, pronounced cheekbones, sad green eyes. Buford had the family cheekbones, but his eyes were brown and more deeply set. Of the two brothers, he had the looks, the bad boy looks.

When he moved across the squeaky floor to the other side of the room, I started breathing again.

"Hello, Daddy," Savannah said to the next man that entered Ida's.

"Savannah," Bull Smike said.

He was a man in his late fifties/early sixties, built like his sons, not so tall, but lanky with broad shoulders. He wore pants and suspenders over a long sleeve white cotton shirt without a tie. He'd left his hat and coat on the porch.

"There are ladies present, boys," he said.

His sons removed their hats. Eustace stuffed his under his poncho. Buford dropped his on a nearby chair seat.

"Miss," he said to me and nodded.

I nodded my head and maintained the eye contact that he had initiated.

His left eye was as milky white as an opal—a cataract was my guess—so he favored his right eye and cocked his head to give his good eye preference. He had dark and healthy, longish hair that was just starting to gray, and a forehead that was deeply wrinkled.

When the door opened briefly behind Savannah's

father, it seemed I was the only person in the room that gave it any notice. A man in a wide-brimmed hat leaned in, looked around, closed the door, and remained outside.

"Why don't you sit over there, Savannah," Bull Smike said in a slow, quiet Ozark drawl, indicating a table across the room near where Buford stood.

"Yes, Daddy," she said and did as she was told.

Otis chose that moment to come from the kitchen area.

Eustace and Buford brought their left hands across to grasp the barrels of the shotguns they held. The weapons were still pointed at the floor, but the brothers were an important step forward if they needed to use them.

"Are you the man who brought Savannah home?" Bull Smike asked Otis.

"I am."

"I want to thank you for that, but I need to speak with my daughter first."

"Take your time," Otis said. "We'll order some breakfast."

"Please do," the older man said and went over and sat with and began speaking softly to Savannah.

Otis sat down with me and hitched his eyebrows as if to say "what next?"

Ida came from the kitchen with fresh coffee and took our orders.

The Smike men were big and strapping, but Otis was truly a large, confident man that could not be intimidated. It was understandable that the bodyguards would not relax until it was clear that he was no threat, but wasn't the real issue why Bull Smike needed that kind of protection? Why should two people who gave Savannah a ride from Oklahoma City be deemed dangerous?

Of course, we were not privy to Savannah's phone conversation with her father earlier that morning. Who knows what she may have said? I didn't see her as a duplicitous person, but with such a childlike personality, what might her interpretation have been of certain events she'd witnessed?

And then there was the simplest explanation, and the most obvious, Bull Smike was a bootlegger and no doubt had enemies. Who was to say who those enemies were and when or where they might strike?

Otis and I were well into our breakfasts when we heard a commotion on the café porch. A woman was shouting Savannah's name.

Savannah stood so quickly her father had to catch his coffee cup to keep it from spilling. "Mama," Savannah called out.

Bull Smike shook his head and gave Eustace a resigned wave of his hand to take care of the matter. But Eustace was unable to do more than back away as the door flew open and a wild-eyed woman in a drenched housedress burst in.

Here was the Irish blood that had birthed the Smike children, the thick red hair, the flashing green eyes, the flaming temper. She advanced on Eustace and struck him in the face with an open-handed right cross that Sugar Ray would have respected.

"How dare you drive off and leave me," she spat at her son, who stood an easy eighteen inches taller than she.

He held his hand up to keep her from hitting him again and stepped back.

"Bronagh," Bull Smike muttered.

"I'll get to you," she said to her husband without giving him a glance, and moved toward Buford, her bare feet leaving muddy size five prints.

Buford held his shotgun behind his leg and his other hand out straight in front of him to keep distance between him and his mother. She slapped his hand several times in anger and frustration as he backed away from her.

"Don't give me that face, Buford James. You can hold me off now, but you won't always be watching."

Frustrated, she picked up a ketchup bottle and hurled it through a window.

"Bronagh," Bull Smike said again, as broken glass clattered to the floor.

She stepped inside Buford's arm and almost punched him in the stomach, but he blocked it. "You wipe that look off your face. You'll get it, boy. Count on it. You'll get it when you least expect it."

"It weren't the daddy they was afraid of," Otis whispered.

I nodded my agreement, wondering what we would do if she came at us.

"Mama," Savannah said and rushed to her mother.

11

BRONAGH AND HER daughter were about the same size, but the mother could have been a big bear with a tiny cub the way she took that girl in her arms and held her. Mama Bear's venomous glances promised violence as she surveyed the room over her cub's shoulder. The silence was deadly.

The outside man that watched from the open doorway dropped his gaze, stepped back, and closed the door when her attention moved toward him.

Bull Smike said, "Eustace, see your mother and sister home."

"Do you have any clothes with you, sweetheart?" Bronagh asked.

Savannah shook her head no.

"Just Ida's apron and the clothes on your back?" Bronagh said, staring at her husband.

"That's all, Mama."

She walked her daughter to the door that Eustace had opened for them, stopped there, and again fixed her eyes on her husband.

"I tore a fender off your new truck, Luther."

He shrugged. "The roads are slippery."

"And something's dragging underneath."

"It's not important," he said, but the brow he wrinkled failed to confirm that sentiment.

"Come on, sweetheart," she said to Savannah in a gentle, loving voice. "We're going home now."

She led her out the door, and the calm that descended on the room made me realize the rain had turned to a sprinkle. The storm had passed.

Bull Smike got to his feet and addressed Buford. "Wait outside."

Buford glanced our direction, but moved at once to obey his father. When we were alone, the older man walked over and pulled a chair around to sit near us.

"Luther?" the café owner said.

She stood near the kitchen door.

"Yes, Ida?"

"I need to put something over that window before the rain spoils my floor."

"Certainly. Come ahead."

Ida advanced with a broom and dustpan. A man in an apron followed her with a large square of cardboard.

"I don't mean to be a bother," she said.

"Please, Ida. Tell Waller Hardware what you need. Send the bill to me." He stuck out his hand. "Luther Smike," he said.

"Otis Millett." Otis shook his hand, and then introduced me.

Bull Smike nodded, but didn't offer his hand. "My daughter says you two saved her life last night. More than once, in fact."

"Well," Otis said. "I don't know if she told you about your son's death. I want to say I'm sorry about that."

Bull Smike sat down. "My son? Oh, you mean Lester."

"Savannah called him her brother."

"He's a second cousin. They was close as little things."

"Uh huh," Otis said.

"We'll claim his body today, bring him home to bury, and find his killer tomorrow or the next day. But I dare say we will find his killer." Bull Smike said.

"We hated leaving him beside the road, but it was Savannah's safety we was concerned with."

"She told me the men who killed Lester tried to kidnap her, but you put a stop to it."

"Well..." Otis said, glancing at me.

"That's how you got your face cut up?"

Otis shrugged.

"Lester did more'n anyone to find out what happened to Savannah."

"What happened to her?" Otis asked.

"She up and left Dallas a few months ago. Just packed a bag and left town."

"Without telling anyone?"

"Not us. Not a word to us. She told the folks at the place where she played piano she was going on a trip. They said she seemed happy."

"So you had someone look into it."

"I drove down and spoke to the police. They couldn't do anything..."

"Without a crime being committed," Otis finished for him.

"That's what they said. And she wasn't really a missing person. We went over to her apartment. It was clear she'd packed a bag."

"That's when you spoke to her place of employment."

"Lester did. He knew somebody over there. He's a... I mean he *was* a musician himself."

"In cowboy bands?" I said.

"You've heard him play, have you, miss?"

"Not really. There was something about him, though."

"He played with Bob Wills now and again," Bull Smike said.

"He must have been good," Otis said.

"He was. He knew folks, too. That's how we found out she'd gone up somewhere near Amarillo."

"Was it a job offer or was she taking a vacation with a boyfriend maybe?" Otis ventured.

Bull Smike glanced over at Ida. She had stretched out the broken window job as long as she could because of her curiosity.

"About finished, Luther," she said.

Otis and I had a few more bites of breakfast as Ida and her helper picked up their tools and mess and headed for the kitchen.

It was indicative of Bull Smike's reputation that the café had not had another customer since the arrival of his clan.

When he felt we were alone, he said, "If you don't mind, Mr. Millett, what is your line of work?"

"My partner and I are private investigators."

He hadn't expected that. After a moment, he said, "Is that so?"

"Yes, sir. The Millett Agency in Fort Worth."

Bull Smike shook his head. "How do you figure into

what happened last evening? Can you clear things up for me?"

"We can try, and maybe you can straighten out some things for us, at the same time."

Otis and Bull Smike talked over the events surrounding Savannah's adventure at Curly's Tavern, and the confrontation with Travis Horner at the Skirvin Hotel.

I wasn't asked to say much, a few things about the men who killed Lester. Mostly I listened as the events of last night were rehashed.

Otis brought it to a halt before an hour had passed.

"We'll be glad to talk some more later, but now we need some sleep."

"Of course you do," Bull Smike said, and insisted on paying our check.

It was midmorning, still overcast, and the rain had almost given it up by the time we left Ida's. Otis and I agreed to meet with the bootlegger again after we'd had some rest. He consigned us to the care of his oldest son, Buford.

We followed his pickup truck down a road through the trees to the Yellow Pines Motel, where he motioned for us to wait in our car while he went into the office. He came out with our keys, gave them to me through the car window, and pointed to the little duplex bungalow down at the end that was ours.

As we drove away, Otis said, "He jabbers as much as Loretta, don't he?"

Loretta was Doc McGraw's wife. She'd been mute most of her adult life, after losing her larynx to the slashing claws of a young mountain lion.

Maybe I said goodnight to Otis before entering my half of the bungalow or maybe I didn't. However, I do remember thinking I should clean my pistol prior to going to bed. But the truth was I didn't get all my clothes off before I fell asleep.

12

THERE WAS A knock on the wall.

"Lee," I said. "Is that you?"

I shook my head and looked around. My watch said 3:30. The window said daytime through the light cotton drapes.

It took me a moment to get my bearings. Small clean room, rustic furniture, my unopened overnight bag in the chair by the table.

I finally knew where I was and who had tapped on the wall.

I knocked back at Otis, finished undressing, and got into the shower. The hot water felt wonderful, except the wound on my arm stung like the devil was chewing on me. I needed to pay attention to that. Otis had some stuff.

I also had a few aches and pains and a bruise on my butt from the hard bounce I'd taken on the highway. As I had a look at it in the mirror, I realized that besides me, only Lee would have ever seen that.

I liked Lee's concern for me. I had never made an effort to explain how well I could take care of myself, but he said once he had an idea from the weapons I carried that I knew what I was doing. Though it didn't keep him from worrying.

I always told him that Otis did all the risky work at our agency.

Uh huh.

I opened the motel room door to the strong scent of pine and the chatter of countless birds. It was sunny and humid.

Otis and I were presentable in fresh clothes. I wore black Levi's so as not to surprise anyone. As usual, my partner was dressed for church: three-piece dark gray suit and tie, fresh dark gray fedora.

Luther Bull Smike and Buford were standing in mottled light near the motel office talking with the manager. They were waiting for us to appear and started toward us when we did. The father was dressed as we'd last seen him. His oldest son had shed his rain gear and was in Levi's and a t-shirt. He was well built.

We put our overnight bags in the trunk of the Buick, and Otis left the lid up and got out a cloth sack of first aid items.

"Let's take care of that arm right now," he said.

"With an audience?"

"Wha'd'you care? That's why you have on a t-shirt, ain't it?" He was right. "Lemme help with your jacket."

"Mornin'," Bull Smike said.

"Gentlemen," Otis said. "We'll just be a minute. My partner took a close one last night and we ain't had a chance to tend to it."

Otis laid my Levi's jacket aside as I pulled my sleeve over my shoulder and tucked it out of the way. The Smikes had a good look at my wound before Otis turned back with some medication to smear on it.

"It's gonna sting," he said.

In fact, it hurt like hell, but Buford and I had locked eyes so I didn't show it.

"The man who killed Lester, he shot at you?" Bull Smike asked, tilting his head, staring, unblinking, with his one good eye.

"He and his partner both did," I said, as Otis bandaged my arm. "One carried a .44 and the other a .357. I don't know which did this."

"I want the names of those men, Miss. I want to meet them personally."

"Get in line," I said, and Buford's frozen face cracked a grin.

There was a picnic area near the motel cabins nestled back among the tall pines with a couple of rough wood tables and benches. After Otis helped me on with my jacket, we walked over. I was starting to like the fresh, clean smell of the place.

Buford brought some cold bottles of beer from his truck for the four of us and opened them on the edge of a table.

Beer for breakfast.

Otis and Buford lit up, and we all stood around like at a company outing, not knowing each other in this environment, but willing to try.

"How long was Savannah gone?" Otis asked, snapping closed his lighter.

"We lost touch with her," Bull Smike said and looked at his son.

"It's been close to four months since we talked to her last," Buford said.

Lo and behold, he speaks.

He went on in that slow Ozark drawl that I was starting to like, "Lester called a short while back and told us he'd located her. We don't have all the details yet. Savannah'll tell us."

The father said, "She has a wonderful memory. You just have to ask the right questions."

"Along about the first of the year she up and moved away?" Otis said.

"Travis Horner took her away," Buford said.

"We know now that's what happened," Bull Smike said. "She went with him to play piano at his restaurant club down the road a spell from Amarillo. She said he was nice to her, but he wouldn't let her leave when she asked to come home."

I said, "Or use the telephone, either, I guess."

No one dealt with that.

"How'd she get away?" Otis asked.

"Lester pulled that off," Bull Smike said.

Buford filled in the details. "Lester got his band a job playing at Horner's place. Only for a few days, but it was enough time to get her out of there."

"How'd the Oklahoma City police end up with her?" Otis asked.

Before he answered, Buford toed aside the pine needles, stepped on his cigarette, picked up the butt, and field stripped it like a military man. "The way I put it together, Lester and his band boys had a station wagon, just enough room for them and their equipment. So he got Savannah over to Amarillo and onto a Greyhound. The deal being, he was to pick her up at the bus station in Oklahoma City."

"The police were waiting at the depot," Otis said.

"I reckon the police boys you ran into at that old tavern, was the ones that got her," Bull Smike said.

"And my partner and I think they work for Travis Horner," Otis said.

"I've got a copper or two here and there tucked away myself," Bull Smike admitted, and then stepped away from the table and turned to face us. "Let me say right off my wife ain't alone in blaming me for giving Savannah some breathing room. Not everyone in my family agreed when I let her go."

"Come on, Dad," Buford said. "They don't need to hear this."

"No, I want these good folks to understand."

Buford and Otis lit cigarettes.

"Some'll tell you my only daughter didn't get every-thing the Lord promised her. I say that ain't true. He saw fit to keep her young in some ways, I'll give you that, but that's no reason, no reason at all, to lock a person up."

He took a deep breath and nodded his head for a moment.

"She run off now and again as she was growin' up. She was just lucky she got home safe from those times. When she got full-grown she needed her own life the same as the rest of us. Bronagh and I fussed over it, but I would not keep Savannah stuck away at home like some kind of circus thing. I knew folks talked...never to my face, mind you, and never within earshot of her brothers..."

Several tiny birds distracted us. The brazen things flittered about our table and darted away, strays from the noisy chorus above us.

"And yet..." he continued, "And yet, I knew, too, that lettin' her go included the chance a vulgar man like Travis Horner might wander by. But ain't that chance true for every young girl out on her own? She wasn't booted from the nest, you understand, devil take the hindmost, none of that. I talked to my girl like any daddy would. It was Savannah told me what she wanted to do. Ain't that so, Buford?"

Buford lifted his hand and shook his head. He didn't want in.

Bull Smike went on.

"We found her a nice place to live in Fort Worth. Lester found her a job where she could make her music. We drove over to visit from time to time. And there she was, free to live her life without being treated like a baby. I knew without her mother hovering over her she'd snap out of that young girl business. I was right, too. When we visited, she told us about her new friends and the fun she was having where she played her music. She was doin' just fine until Travis Horner butted in."

"She's home now," Otis said.

"Yes. You brought her home, and we are in your debt, sir."

"You don't owe us a thing," Otis said, and stepped forward to shake Bull Smike's hand. "We was happy to do it."

My partner was trying to wrap it up.

"I'll tell you what we owe you," Buford said. "A case of our best Kentucky Bourbon for punching Travis Horner in the face. I'll get it for you now, if you'll open the trunk of your car."

Otis laughed and tossed me his keys. I walked over

with Bull Smike's oldest son who got the bourbon and put it in the trunk of the Buick.

When we were alone, I said, "You don't think your sister should be out on her own, do you?"

He was a moment looking me in the eye, but when he did I saw intelligence there and caring.

"Bull doesn't want to accept how she is."

"How much more bad has to happen to her?"

"Because she's his, she has to be perfect."

"How come you stay here? You've been away in the military, haven't you?"

He gave me a hard stare.

"You pretty much ask whatever you please, don't you?"

"You don't have to answer."

He closed the trunk lid, and said, "We weren't introduced."

"Kristin Van Dijk," I said, and stuck out my hand.

He took my hand in his.

"Buford James Smike," he said, and smiled.

Bad boy looks with a smile that could break a girl's heart. I was obligated to smile back.

We shook hands, perhaps a shade longer than Emily Post would've thought proper. And, of course, I thought about Lee.

13

OTIS SAID, "BULL Smike and Travis Horner run the two biggest bootlegging concerns in Oklahoma. Did you know that?"

We were on the road to Fort Worth.

"Not till just now," I said.

"Both are family operations. Bull controls eastern Oklahoma. Horner services the west. There're some little guys in the mix, but the big guns are Horner and Smike."

"Who has Oklahoma City?" I asked.

"They squabble over that."

"What fun would it be without something to squabble over?"

"He hired us to find the shooters," Otis said.

"Old man Smike?"

"Yep."

"We don't need to be hired," I said. "We're gonna do that anyway."

"Couldn't talk him out of it."

"Otis...?"

"Yeah?"

"What do you make of Savannah not using the telephone?"

"How do you mean?"

"Why not give the folks a call? She had no trouble at the filling station yesterday morning."

"You're right. Does seem strange, but maybe Horner was keeping her from it."

"He was keeping her all right. That diamond is small, but the setting is platinum."

"The ring, you mean."

"The earrings, too."

"Platinum, huh? So he was spending money on her."

"Horner splits his time between Dallas and Amarillo, doesn't he? I mean, we see him at the fights some times."

"His family's legit business is in the city. Their bootleg operation is up on the high plains for a straight shot into western Oklahoma."

"So, when he was going back and forth between the family business in Dallas and his bootleg interests in Amarillo, he was leaving Savannah playing piano at his roadhouse in Amarillo."

"Sounds right to me."

"Why didn't she pack up one morning and walk away, or at least phone home?"

Otis shook his head. "She didn't do neither one of them things, did she?"

"Not that we've heard about."

We were silent for a mile or so, and then I said, "She stays in Amarillo four months without a peep. Hard to figure that one."

"A lawyer I know likes to say, twelve men, twelve agendas."

"That's the truth."

"And, don't forget, Missy..."

"I know. I know. It's got nothing to do with us anyway."

"Right as rain. We was hired to do a job. We did it."

"And now Savannah Smike is somebody else's concern," I said.

"Don't go there, Missy. The fact is, this Smike and Horner fracas ain't got nothin' to do with us."

"There's the big question. How did Bull Smike's daughter get in between the two most powerful bootleggers in Oklahoma?"

"You can't leave it alone, can you?"

Otis was right. I needed to let it go.

And then he said, "There's one more thing, though."

"Yes?" I said.

"What do you think three P's means?"

"Three P's? The letter P?"

"Yeah. P-P-P. Bull Smike says that's who bootleggers have to pay off to stay in business."

"Police," I ventured.

"Yeah, and politicians and what about the last P?"

Otis let it hang for a minute while he dragged out a Lucky and lit up.

Finally, he said, "Police, Politicians, and Preachers."

I should have been surprised, maybe, but I wasn't. Each P had its own reasons for wanting the state to stay dry and bootleg money helped support those reasons—good or bad, right or wrong.

The Millett Agency did business from an office/apartment above a Chinese restaurant in a nondescript brick building in a blue-collar section of Fort Worth. It was early evening when we parked in the dirt lot behind the building, cut through the kitchen of the Mandarin Palace, and climbed the back stairs.

When we entered the office, Otis took the case of whiskey into the other room before coming back and heading for the kitchen area.

"I'm making a pot of coffee," he said, and fired up a Lucky.

I had already gone over to the hook board and gotten some car keys.

My partner was focused. "That's what I hate about travel. You can never get a decent cuppa joe."

The cleaning lady had come while we were gone. She'd left a window cracked and the old floor fan running. As a result, the place was close to odorless. But it hardly mattered. Otis started manufacturing odors as fast as he could.

"I'm taking the Mercury," I said.

"Why face an empty apartment? Stay here tonight. We can go downstairs, have some supper."

"Thanks, but I think I'll grab something at Wally's, shoot a few games, and hit the sack."

"You and Lee ever gonna make up?"

He'd been good about not getting involved. Why now?

I started for the door.

"What's it been, since March?"

"We have some things to work out, Otis. See you tomorrow."

14

MY APARTMENT WAS upstairs from Wally's, a serious pool hall with regulation nine-foot tables in a commercial section of Fort Worth. Wally, the owner, had a lunch counter and newsstand, too. He and his wife Maude had lived above their business for fifteen years before I settled in.

A few years back, they'd decided to buy a Victorian farmhouse set on a six-acre avocado orchard down near Waxahachie. Wally told me this was the beginning of their retirement. Maude was going to stay home with the orchard and the cats, and Wally was going to make the drive for a few years before selling out.

When I learned about their plans, I spoke to her. She spoke to him, and they let me rent the place.

"We knew your dad," Maude had said.

"You're here shooting pool all the time, anyway," Wally had added.

There were two entrances to the spacious apartment, one through the pool hall and the other off the alley. The enclosed stairway that went up the outside wall at the end of the building started inside a two-car garage and led to the apartment's kitchen door.

Having that back entrance helped keep my comings and goings private, and being able to go down to the pool hall when I felt like it was appealing, too.

Wally said, "That Oklahoma twister get anywhere near where you was?"

"Nah. Not even close."

"That's good. We worried. They showed pictures on the news. It was flipping cars over. Made a house disappear. Maude said the house went to Kansas."

"I'll take pickles on that burger."

"Oh, yeah. Let me get that off the griddle," he said and hustled over to the grill where my burger and bun were smoking.

Otis and I tried to describe Wally one time and decided he had an average older guy look, perfect for someone who wanted to disappear in a crowd.

I was sitting on a stool at the short end of the L-shaped lunch counter so I could see the room. There was the kid who was always there reading magazines he couldn't afford to buy. Wally didn't care. "Better he's in here reading than out there getting in trouble."

There were the regulars and a good-sized group of others at the tables. I saw one guy who looked like he wanted to play. I watched his game for a while.

Wally came back with my burger. "Burnt the bun a little. I scraped it.'

"It's okay."

"I'll make another if you want."

"It's fine, Wally. And a Dr Pepper."

He went to the ice chest. "While you was gone I saw lights on upstairs. Saw Lee's car, so I knew it was okay."

"Not a problem," I said.

He put my pop on the counter. "You and Lee ever gonna make up?"

Jesus.

"We're talking."

"It's been a month or longer."

"I know. Let's see how it goes."

"We like Lee."

"Me, too. Say, do you know that fella in the green shirt?"

He looked. "Table three?"

"Uh huh."

"Not really."

"You think he has any money?"

Wally chuckled. "You remind me of your daddy sometimes, except he never had a steady job like you. I'm closing in an hour and a half."

As I ate my dinner, I watched the guy some more, and had a look at his cue. He'd brought it with him. I glanced around for his case and spied the beat up leather thing across the room leaning against the wall behind a chair, almost hidden by his jacket that was thrown over the arm of the chair. I had a look at his khaki pants and worn-in, high-top work shoes. He was a traveling man.

My grifter friend, Harlan, told me that gamblers will ignore any sign that stands in the way of them losing their money.

It sure was true of Warren, the guy I'd been watching at table three. When I approached him to shoot some nine ball for cash, guys in the place began drifting over. After we got past me being female and he agreed to play, the crowd left us room, but made a kind of wall around our table. Wouldn't a sane guy have changed his mind at that point?

Unless he was confident he wouldn't lose.

Or didn't care. Harlan again.

We established the bet and agreed to alternate breaks.

"Loser racks," he said.

I shrugged. "Where're you from, Warren?"

He had an accent I couldn't place.

"Around," he said.

"Haven't seen you before."

He didn't say anything.

"I know most of the players in town," I said.

"A town this size. I doubt it."

"I should have said *good* players. Are you a good player, Warren?"

"Why don't you stop your yakkin' and find out?" he said.

That made the crowd hoot. "Grudge match," someone said. But that mob knew me and as soon as we started playing, they grew silent.

We lagged for first break. I won, sank three on the break, and ran the table. He tossed his money in a corner pocket. He broke next and ran the table. I put my money in a side pocket. The winner of the game we were going to play in just over an hour would win it all.

Warren was a sourpuss and self-assured and could shoot nine ball. He had a steady stroke and could leave the cue ball where he wanted it. We played several quick games, trading wins, mostly sinking on the breaks, and running the table. The crowd was being entertained by some clean pool shooting.

He was a slim guy in his twenties, five-eight or -nine, with a light brown, very short crew cut that started way up his skull. He had a narrow head and dark, quick eyes and eyebrows too thick for his face. Come to think of it, his nose didn't work for his face either; the bridge was too flat, too wide. He was like a mongrel, with thin lips that never smiled. And he had a scar on his jaw that seemed too red to me. I considered myself knowledgeable when it came to facial scars.

I became less interested in his game than his looks. The more I studied him, the more convinced I became that Warren was wearing a disguise; a damned good one, but he wasn't who he wanted us to see. He was like me when I was in my horn-rimmed clear eyeglasses and wig.

Warren wanted to be remembered with receding short hair and heavy eyebrows and a fresh scar on his jaw, because later he would have a full head of hair, normal eyebrows, no scar, and maybe he would be wearing glasses.

The skin crawled at the back of my neck.

Armed robbers had Warren's kind of don't-give-a-damn confidence.

At the end of the next game I won, I said, "I'm thirsty. Buy you a beer or a coke or something?"

Mister Confidence shook his head, put his money in the corner pocket, and began racking the balls.

Several guys wandered over with me.

Wally was cleaning his kitchen area. He stopped to serve them beers and got me a Dr Pepper. After the others had paid and walked away, I whispered, "Wally, this guy's cue case is against the far wall behind the chairs there. You see it?"

Wally looked and nodded yes.

"It's standing up a little too straight for an old leather case, don't you think?"

"Now that you mention it," Wally said.

"I think there's a shotgun in there. Can you make your way over with a broom or something, without anyone noticing, and check that out?"

Wally glanced at Warren, brought his eyes back to me, and nodded yes. "What if you're right?"

"Unload it and put it back the way you find it. Can you do that?"

"If you keep the crowd staring at the table, I can."

"Good," I said, and walked away carrying my Dr Pepper.

Wally had been in business and had dealt with the public for a long time. He'd seen armed robbers before, so I felt certain he knew what was going on. There's no law against carrying a shotgun in a cue case. That gun has to come out of there and be used as a threat before the law can step in.

I hadn't finished my soda pop before Wally was moving around turning out the lights above the tables that weren't being used. Where we were playing, in the center of the darkening room, became an oasis of light as he performed a normal part of his closing-time ritual.

When it was 9:40, I had just won a game and Warren was racking the balls for our final game. I was armed and felt I could take care of things if it got violent, as I suspected it might. My suspicions were based on premonition, but I would rather apologize for flawed intuition than take a chance with the lives of my pool hall friends and the kid still reading magazines.

We lagged for the final game; I won, and ran the table. Anything could have gone wrong, but it didn't, and the place went nuts when I dropped the last ball. One of the regulars dug the money out of the corner pocket and began counting it aloud. Somebody else dragged my money from the side pocket and tidied it up to give back to me.

I called out, "Hey, everyone. It's closing time now, but come back tomorrow night and the beers are on me until we've spent all of Warren's money."

That made everyone happy. They jeered and laughed as they gathered their belongings and headed for the door where Wally stood, ready to lock up after the last customer left.

I stepped out of the light, pulled my .38, and jacked in a round with my back to where I knew Warren was returning from getting his jacket and cue case.

I turned back to face the lighted area without moving into it, keeping my pistol behind my leg. In my other hand, I pinched in plain view the two stacks of money I had been given; a little something for misdirection in case I needed it.

"Who do we have left, Kristin?" Wally called out from the door.

"Just Warren," I said. "Lock up. I think he wants to talk."

I heard the double dead bolts on the front door thud into place as Warren came toward me around the edge of the circle of light. By his side, in a relaxed hand, he held a sawed-off shotgun. A lanyard dangled from an eyebolt screwed into the chopped-off stock so the stubby weapon could be hung from his shoulder under a coat.

Our boy was all business.

My heartbeat cranked up a notch. "You a sore loser, Warren?"

"Tell him to unlock the front door."

I didn't say or do anything. He leveled his shotgun at me.

"Tell him or it's gonna get nasty."

"You'll break your wrist if you fire that with one hand."

"What's going on?" Wally asked as he walked up to us.

"Crybaby wants his money back."

Wally reached over, snatched the money from me, and started for his office. "I'll just put that in the safe."

Warren raised his voice. "Stop right there, Old Man."

Wally ignored him and walked on.

Warren pumped his gun to chamber a shell and brought it down on the pool hall owner. "I said stop."

Wally kept walking and Warren squeezed the trigger. Click.

He looked stunned.

He glanced at me, pumped the gun, and tried again. Click.

He'd made his point.

I shot him in the knee.

He cried out and fell back, his arms flailing. His elbow hit hard against a table edge and sent his shotgun clattering across the floor. As he collapsed, I stepped forward and drop kicked him in the face.

"Sorry to muss your makeup," I said.

Wally came back over, the money still in his fist. "You okay?"

"Yeah. Stay out of the light. There's somebody outside. That's why he wanted the door unlocked."

"Uh huh," Wally said, and looked toward the front.

"It's time to call the police," I said.

"Did that already," Wally allowed.

A few moments later there was pounding at the front door, and we saw brightly colored patrol car lights.

"Better let 'em in before they break my glass."

As he walked away, I said, "Stick that money in your pocket, Wally, or the cops'll take it as evidence."

I looked down at Warren, the would-be killer of my friend.

He was in pain, seated awkwardly, supporting himself with a stiff arm, the knee of his khaki pants dark with blood. His nose was bleeding, too. He was staring at me with his good eye, the one that wasn't swelling shut.

"You cunt," he said.

What would Otis do?

What the hell. I kicked him again, that time in his injured knee.

Dialing the police wasn't Wally's only independent action. The busybody's other phoning efforts included ringing up Detective Lee Pierson.

It rubbed me the wrong way at first, but I have to admit it was nice to see the handsome guy crossing the poolroom looking worried about me. Like Wally and Otis had pointed out, it had been a few weeks.

And because I was the reason a respected Dallas detective made an appearance at a Fort Worth crime scene, I was shown professional courtesy and didn't have to go downtown until the next day to reclaim my weapon and provide a formal statement.

When things were all wrapped up at his place of business, Wally turned out the lights, locked the front door from the outside, and left us there in the dark.

Lee and I talked for a while and, of course, ended up stretched out on a table, kissing. That caused him to decide, given that I'd suffered the trauma of an armed robbery attempt, that it might be wise if he kept an eye on me.

"Psychological reactions are the rage these days," he said, holding me in his arms.

"I read that article," I said, snuggling closer.

"Uh huh, well, I wouldn't want you to be alone if you should…"

"Suddenly find myself suffering from a psychological reaction?"

"Exactly."

"Mmmm. We should probably go upstairs, then."

"The better to keep an eye on you?"

"You just never know," I said.

"That's the thing, isn't it? We should play it safe."

"If you think so," I said.

15

LATE THE NEXT day, as I entered the office, Otis said, "I talked to Wally."

"Oh, yeah?"

"Trouble follows you sure as night follows day. Never seen nothing like it."

"Oh, don't get carried away," I said. "I'm not present at every armed robbery in the city, and there are plenty of them."

"It was a good thing you was at that one or we'd be gettin' spiffied up to go to Wally's funeral."

The room felt close. I took off my jacket and hung it on the tree by the door.

"Is the fan on high?" I asked.

"Is now," Otis said, his chair squeaking as he leaned over and hit the switch. "See you got your piece back. What did the boys downtown say?"

"There'll be an inquiry, but the D.A.'s office says not to worry. Warren and his buddy have done a string of these."

I pulled a Dr Pepper from our little Frigidaire.

"Where'd they catch the accomplice?"

"In their car out front."

"Put up a fight?"

"Nah, he was tuned into Villa Acuna. Where's the church key?"

"On the cabinet the last I saw of it. He was just sittin' out front of Wally's listening to the radio?"

"He was high on wacky weed, forgot which side was up," I said.

"Another Einstein."

I found the bottle opener under the coffee container lid, screwed the lid on the coffee jar, and opened my drink.

"They're wanted for murder in five states," I told Otis.

"Is that a fact? Five states. You're quite the hero. Or, what is it for gals?"

"Heroine."

"Yeah. Any reward money out there?"

I didn't bother to answer that. I said, "I read an article called "Psychology and Crime" that said defense attorneys have started calling these kinds of guys psychopaths. They can't help themselves."

"What're you talking about? They tried to kill you and Wally."

"Yeah, but it's not really their fault, see."

"Well, they can call 'em psychopaths if they want, but if they screw up in Texas we'll show 'em whose fault it is. I'll pull the switch myself if they run short of help over at the prison."

"You seem a little wound up."

He rose from his cluttered desk to get a fresh cup of coffee, if fresh can be used in reference to the sludge he drank.

"While you've been lollygaggin' the day away downtown with Fort Worth's finest, I've been lining up our next job."

"And that put you in a bad mood?"

"Well, you know, it's a gal who's got her underpants in a twist over the man she just divorced. Wants protection. Baby sitting's more like it."

"We're bodyguards now?"

"No, no, but I couldn't just hang up in her ear."

"He made threats, the ex-husband?"

"She said no. Then convinced a judge to issue a court order that forbids the ex from coming anywhere near her."

"That's clever," I said. "He'll be in contempt if he disobeys."

Otis heaved a sigh. "She was a handful on the phone, afraid of him, hates him, never wants to see him again."

"It's getting late. You gonna get back in time to go to the fights?"

"That's what has me riled up."

"Ahhhh, okay, now I get it. Call her back. Tell her something has come up. You'll see her tomorrow morning."

"Could you do that for me, Missy? Could you call her back and make my excuse? I ain't at my best with hysterical women."

I stepped over to the desk. His face looked better after a night's sleep. It was still obvious he'd been in a hassle, but the bruising and swelling around his eye was almost gone.

He pushed a scrap of paper at me. "Here's her name and number."

"I'll make the call, but you owe me dinner after the fights," I said.

I can't remember ever seeing the ceiling at the old Civic Auditorium. Though I was sure it was up there somewhere beyond the tobacco smoke and steaming lights and blaring speakers that formed the canopy above the square of canvas where the fights happened on Friday nights.

The scents and sounds made the place exciting. Besides the sluggers, it was the crush of fans milling about that guaranteed the fights were a spectacle. The men were of all ages, but mostly Otis' generation. They spoke loudly and didn't care who heard them. They wore suits and ties and hats, smoked long cigars, and came from every walk of life, rich and poor, with one thing in common: love of the sweet science.

The women were outnumbered and reveled in it. They were fearless dames who had been up the street and back, held their perfect hairdos high, and would look you right in the eye while you studied their exaggerated makeup. They strutted about to be noticed in their colorful fitted dresses, sheer nylons, and spiked heels.

And, believe me, they were noticed. A jealous man would have been reduced to suicide in the face of the numberless rude whistles and crude sounds and comments thick with overtone.

My dad took me to the fights from the time I was little. He wanted me to love the sport as much as he did. And how curious it was, the fights being a wordless game and my dad such a lover of words.

Otis and I rarely missed the Friday Night Fights.

"There he is," I said.

"Hard to miss that dandy, ain't it?" Otis said.

Reggie 'Sidecar' Sanchez could've passed for the

handsome Cesar Romero if he'd been a foot taller and ten years older. The custom tailored, light wool suit he wore that evening was pale ivory, his silk shirt soft orange with matching tie and kerchief. Naturally, his shoes were Italian.

Here it was the women watching a man as he held court near the front row of seats at the edge of the apron surrounding the ring. Sidecar was always up front. It was smart business for a bookie to be easy to find.

R.J., Sidecar's omnipresent assistant, was an ex-welterweight with a scarred brow and an ear like mine to prove it. A blue collar kind of guy, he carried the pencil and notebook. No one ever directly addressed R.J., but he heard everything and wrote down the bets as they were laid down to his boss.

The money went to an inside pocket of Sidecar's immaculate jacket.

"Mister Millett," Sidecar said, giving my partner's cut face the once over.

He never acknowledged me and I wasn't certain why. Otis had quit introducing me, since it seemed pointless to do so.

I used to think when I dressed for the fights that by wearing nicely cut black slacks, pretty blouses, and a black Bolero jacket maybe Sidecar would see me. But that apparently wasn't the key. Maybe he found fault with my black snakeskin boots.

"Evening, Reggie," Otis said. "Everything going right for you?"

"Splendidly, thank you. What can I do for you? You haven't begun to wager again, have you?"

Sidecar spoke in a voice as clipped and manicured as his nails, a trained manner of speech, perhaps to hide any trace of his Hispanic background.

"You'll be the first to know if I do."

"How kind of you." He glanced about. "Before we form a line, what can I do for you?"

Sidecar had a sharp eye and a keen memory for faces and names. Otis put that to use from time to time.

"I'm looking for the name of a shooter, Reggie. A dangerous young man, tall Gary Cooper-type build. Has a big smile. Runs with an older guy, a driver."

"And why do you think I might know him?"

"Maybe this shooter's been talkin' to Travis Horner," Otis said.

Sidecar started to respond, then paused.

"There could be some cash," Otis said.

He must've been thinking of Bull Smike.

"It's never about money with us, Mister Millett. How-ever, there is something included in an estate sale that has come to my attention. From the library, a six-volume set on modern architecture. If I show interest, the price will skyrocket."

Sidecar Sanchez had one business: making book, and one passion: architecture.

"Books?" Otis said.

"I've seen them," I said to Otis. "They're at C. Bell's Rare Books. They're first edition, very nice condition."

At that moment I learned what was meant by a pregnant pause. Sidecar, Otis, and R.J. all stared at me. I returned the bookie's gaze.

Reggie 'Sidecar' Sanchez's first words to me: "And you would know about this for what reason?"

"She reads everything," Otis said, as a matter of fact.

"Respectfully...she can speak for herself," Sidecar said.

Now it was my partner's turn to be ignored.

"Well," I said, "I've grown tired of these hyperbolic paraboloids and worse that are sprouting up all over the place in the name of architecture. It's rather pleasant to see good photography of the important structures. I guess that's the reason."

There was a pause, and then Sidecar smiled, shook his head, and spoke to the heavens, "In snakeskin boots, no less."

It *was* the boots.

To Otis, he said, "I may be able to help you."

And to me, he said, "See what you can get Miss Bell to quote you on them and let me know. I'll pay you ten percent if you can get me a civilized price."

16

AFTER THE FIGHTS, to celebrate my breakthrough with Sidecar Sanchez, Otis and I drove over to Sylvia's Steaks, a twenty-four-hour workingman's meat and potatoes place near the stockyards. We wanted to see if we could put on some weight that neither of us needed.

The specialty at Sylvia's was a giant mesquite-grilled porterhouse steak smothered in sweet onions and mushrooms and served with what Otis called killer fried potatoes. Added to that was buttered and grilled sourdough bread and peas and corn and coleslaw.

"I'm full as a tick," I said when we'd finished. "I'm not eating again for a week."

As we were walking out, Otis winked at Sylvia and got an elbow in the ribs.

"Flirt with somebody else," she told him. "I'm a married woman."

"Holy shit," Otis said on the way to the car. "Can't nobody take a jape no more?"

"She's always in a bad mood," I said.

Otis rubbed his ribs. "Bet it's her that wrestles them cows to the ground to get them porterhouses."

I laughed, punched him the ribs on the other side, and ran. There was no catching me, so he shouted, "Lookin' to walk home, are you?"

"What's the matter?" I called back. "You can't take a jape?"

We were in the Buick and several blocks away from Sylvia's before Otis mentioned that we were being followed. I didn't look back. I put one in the chamber of my.38 and placed it in my lap, opened my window, and glanced at the time: 11:23.

"Know the make?" I asked.

"Newish, I'd guess. Strong battery, bright lights."

"Keeping cars between us?"

"Uh huh. Let's take some turns. We'll see."

It was Friday night and we were on a main thoroughfare, so there was plenty of traffic, especially young people, shouting out their windows, screeching their tires, gunning their engines, and driving too fast. At our next stop, Otis didn't signal, but when the light changed, he hung a right and put the pedal down to gain some distance.

I twisted in my seat and watched. We were almost to the next corner before the car with the hot lights made the turn and there were still cars between us.

Otis turned right again and punched it. Halfway down the block, he braked hard, backed into the dark alley, stopped close to the building on his side, and killed the lights. We waited with the engine running.

If we were being followed, we wouldn't see them until they passed the narrow alley entrance. There was a chance of our being seen, too, but we were in the shadows, the

Buick was dark blue, and we weren't moving.

Two cars cruised by before the one we were waiting for passed. We both spoke up when we saw the new DeSoto. We believed that was the car that was following us. And, even though Otis moved at once, a convertible full of teenage girls got between the new DeSoto and us.

The boys in the car behind us weren't happy about our slipping in from nowhere and shouted and gunned their engine.

"I wanted to tiptoe in, damn it."

The DeSoto turned left and the driver looked over his shoulder at us.

My heart revved up. "It's Ugly."

"Shit!" Otis said, hitting his brakes after just punching his gas.

The boys from behind had whipped up beside us. "Hey, Grandpa," the t-shirted crew cut hanging out the right hand window yelled. "Turn on your lights."

Otis pulled some police tin from his coat pocket and stuck it out toward the kid, whose eyes went wide.

"Get lost," Otis snarled. "Now!"

"Go! Go! Go!" the kid squealed at the driver and their car jumped forward, tires burning marks in the street as they tore away.

As soon as they were clear, Otis whipped the Buick into an accelerating left turn and we began searching for the DeSoto.

"You get the license?" Otis asked a few blocks later, after it was clear we'd lost them.

"Yep," I said. "But six to five it's stolen."

"Then at the first phone booth, let's report it."

We found a late-night drugstore and parked down

the street. I waited in a dark doorway nearby and kept watch while Otis went inside to make the call.

When he was gone longer than I expected, I walked over and looked into the well-lit store through the plate glass window. And there was Otis in his suit and fedora, sitting on a stool at the soda fountain, drinking something red through a straw from a tall glass.

The picture he created was one I would never forget, like one of those Rockwell drawings on a magazine cover.

When he came out, he said, "I feel better. I had a cherry phosphate."

Down the street from the store, near where we parked, we paused in the shadows.

"We should've seen this coming," I said.

"I don't see how, Missy. Makes me wonder what happened on that country road outside Oklahoma City."

"We destroyed their car. The cops were supposed to go out there."

"We don't know what happened, though, do we?"

"It must have gone the shooters' way. Look how fast they got down here."

"And how fast they found us."

"Hell, we're listed in the Yellow Pages. That part didn't take a degree."

"You didn't see who was in the DeSoto with Ugly, did you?"

"I can guess," I said.

"Uh huh. And another good guess is Travis Horner is payin' the expenses. I'll take the blame. I was the one wallowin' with flea-bitten dogs."

"You should've done more damage to Mister Horner."

"A coma, you mean."

"Not a bad idea. We need to make a believer of him."

"There will be a next time, Missy. But here's the thing right now. We ain't got a clue how much these guys are already onto us. They have our office address, and maybe Wally's address, too."

"I've got to give Lee a call."

"He's stayin' with you again?"

"For now," I said.

"Then call him. You ain't goin' home tonight. If they know our habits, they can stake us out and do it from a distance."

"Sniper rifles wouldn't be their game," I said.

"You think Ugly and the tall guy are the only shooters Horner's hired?"

"I'm not liking this."

"We gotta watch it from every angle, Missy. We're being hunted, and till we can turn the tables on these pricks, we can't take nothin' for granted."

"Sidecar Sanchez wasn't the only guy you put the word out to."

"That's true, Missy. But he's the most reliable."

"Somebody'll come back to us," I said. "Somebody's gonna see these guys."

The wise move was to stay the night at Henry Chin's and start fresh tomorrow. I called him from the gas station where we filled up.

"Otis stay in spare room," Henry said. "Maybe bed not fall down. Can't promise."

Henry was glad we were on our way, whatever the reason.

I had grown too busy lately to make the drive, especially with all the time I'd been spending with Lee. Henry and I missed each other. I missed my dog Jim, too.

"Fix big breakfast," Henry said, before hanging up.

Food again.

I hadn't been given the chance to sleep off Sylvia's porterhouse and trimmings and Henry was talking about his country breakfast special.

For reasons known only to him, when he cooked his special, he prepared enough to feed a corral full of hungry ranch hands. Pork chops, eggs, potatoes, onions, okra, *poblano* chilies, biscuits, and gravy made up the basic menu, the larger portion of which would not be eaten until it was dumped into Jim's enamel dishpan.

After a pan full of country breakfast scraps, my big German shepherd was guaranteed a long day of sloth curled up near the cellar door digesting more food than he would normally eat in several days.

But that was ahead of us.

It was better than two hundred miles out to Henry's, but the traffic was light. Abilene slowed us down a little, though most of the way we did between ninety and a hundred.

I saw Jim waiting beneath the jacaranda trees. He'd heard the car when we left the highway and had trotted the quarter mile down from the house to meet us.

"You care if I let him in back?" I asked.

"Have at it," Otis said and pulled over after he turned into Henry's drive.

Jim knows how to behave in a car, but he hadn't seen me for several weeks, so it was Katie bar the door for a few minutes until he got the wiggles and licks out of his system. Otis drove on like nothing was happening, but I'm sure he knew Jim's rough paws and claws were marking his leather upholstery.

At eight the next morning, Henry came out to the hacienda and woke me. Jim had stayed with me. There he was on his rug next to the bed, though he was accustomed to getting up with Henry at sunup. I couldn't love that dog any more if I tried.

"Otis say you sleep all day," Henry called from outside the door. "Come on now. Breakfast almost ready."

I let Jim out and drew a bath in the giant, lion-footed bathtub that sat in plain view at one end of the large rectangular room. Henry built the hacienda for his son Will, but after he and my dad were murdered in the winter of '52, Henry said the hacienda was my home for as long as I wanted it to be.

When I was living out there, I had taken two-hour baths in that tub, staring at the undersides of the cherry-stained roofing tiles, daydreaming about the future. But not today. Today, I hurried.

"What took you so long?" Otis said when I entered the kitchen.

I glanced at the clock: eight-forty. Otis was already seated at the kitchen table, a steaming cup of coffee in front of him, a dishtowel stuck in his collar, a knife in one hand, a fork in the other.

"Hank's been workin' his fingers to the bone. Hope you're hungry."

Henry was dishing up a plate from a skillet and several pots on the stove. I suspected there were biscuits in the oven.

"Bony fingers," Henry said, and gave me his best smile.

Jim sat nearby watching Henry's every move. He was a smart dog and knew that with so much activity in the kitchen, he was bound to come out a winner.

I squeezed a tall glass of orange juice and figured that and a buttered biscuit was going to be my breakfast. I would get some noise about it, but I was going to stick to my guns.

"No breakfast?" Henry asked, because we had lived together long enough for him to know the signs.

"Just juice, thank you."

"You ain't havin' Hank's pork chops?" Otis said.

He didn't pursue it because Henry slipped a heaping plate of food down in front of him. I thought about Otis needing another cherry phosphate as he doused the fried eggs, potatoes, and pork chops with hot sauce.

Five minutes later, holding a full plate, Henry sat down with a dishtowel tucked in his collar and the two farm hands began putting it away.

"I woke up from a dream last night," I said. "I was a long time getting back to sleep."

"Bad dream?" Henry asked.

"Creepy," I said.

"Could you snag the coffee?" Otis said.

"Sure." I brought the coffee over, filled his cup, and then left the pot where he could reach it.

"Tell us," Otis said.

"It's strange really. When I woke up I realized it wasn't just a dream."

"Wha'd'you mean?"

"It was about the Hudson, Otis. The car Lester was driving."

"What about it?"

"The trunk lid was up."

"I ain't followin' this. You had a dream the trunk was open?"

"Yeah, I did. But it really *was* open. When I went back there and found Lester, the trunk lid was up."

"They was looking for something," Otis mumbled while chewing a pork chop.

"Yeah. Exactly. I forgot to mention it the other night. Too much happening."

"That's okay. You remembered it now."

"They wanted Savannah, but they were also looking for something."

"What do you suppose...?" Otis mumbled, waving his fork.

"So now I think the shooters had three jobs. Kill everybody. Bring back Savannah..."

"And bring back something else. Maybe they got it," Otis said.

"Trunk empty?" Henry asked.

"Yeah, it was," I said. "The lid was up and the trunk was empty."

"Something big if put in trunk," he said.

"It implies that, don't it, Hank?"

"The lanky guy wasn't carrying anything when he left Savannah in the grass."

"And right after that you was up tight to the Pontiac," Otis said. "Did you see anything inside the car?"

"Nothing."

"So, maybe they didn't find whatever it was they was lookin' for."

"Change order."

"Do what, Hank?"

"What they look for and killing you more important than woman," Henry said. "Big thing more important than woman."

We stared at Henry for a long moment.

"He could be right," I said. "A new order of importance would be, find the unknown object, kill everyone, grab Savannah."

"Oklahoma killers now in Texas," Henry said. "Why killers here two minutes after you come back? Try this order. Kill you. Get woman. Find big thing."

Henry saw it clearly.

"Maybe easy make woman do things if you dead. Out of way."

"He's a bundle of joy," Otis said.

And smart. He'd run a successful business for twenty-five years while he was learning the language, putting a son through college, and dealing with prejudice.

"That gives us our marchin' orders, now don't it?"

"Do them before they do us," I said.

"I like the sound of that and maybe we'll get our chance to right some wrongs, but we oughta be thinkin' about gettin' the Fort Worth and Dallas forces on our side, too."

"Get serious, Otis. You see these guys rolling over for an arrest?"

"I say they've done time and puttin' 'em back in prison might not be that tough a job with them stealin' cars and carryin' weapons."

"Okay. Maybe Sidecar comes up with a name and we

can get your police plan started, but that doesn't fix the immediate problem."

"You mean the one about stayin' alive," Otis said. "That problem?"

"Stay alive good idea," Henry said, waving his fork too much like Otis.

17

THE SALESMAN AT the big used car lot in Abilene was a weasel. Otis wanted to compare some things and the guy kept flapping his gums.

"Go back inside and stay out of our hair," I told him.

The weasel glanced at Otis.

Otis said, "You heard her. Beat it."

The weasel was too thick-skinned to be embarrassed, but he went inside anyway.

My partner wanted some muscle under the hood as well as a car that could handle his size. After some tire kicking, and leaving a half dozen hoods up, he chose a black 1956 Oldsmobile 98.

The weasel came out to finish the deal, and when he walked up, Otis slapped him so hard the car salesman staggered about for a moment regaining his balance.

"What was that for?" he asked, blinking his eyes and working his jaw.

"That's a love tap. Try screwing me over and see what you get," Otis told him.

Ten minutes later, after getting a fair deal, we drove out in Otis' new car.

It was close to noon when we arrived in Fort Worth.

We drove past our building a couple of times and looked everywhere before Otis dropped me in front and swung around to park in back.

Madame Li tapped at the window. I nodded and stepped inside.

She was our landlady as well as the ruler of the Mandarin Palace. She spent much of her day sitting on a high black lacquered stool between an ancient cash register and the front glass window.

Very little happened on our street or in our building that she didn't see or wasn't told about.

She spoke in confident, flawless English. I had never asked, but I felt certain that she was American born and educated at exclusive schools.

"There is a woman waiting to see your partner." Her glance directed me to a booth midway back. "I've sedated her to some degree with green tea and herbs, but she's in an anxious state and I could only do so much."

"Within the law," I added, and we exchanged a smile.

"Will Otis enter from the back?"

"Yes," I said, and Madame Li gave some quick instructions in Chinese to a waiter who went directly to the kitchen.

Madame Li always wore the latest fashion. She was partial to Chanel and complimented the designer's clothes with her slim figure, glowing complexion, and impeccable hair and makeup.

"You ever get the feeling that the Mandarin Palace is a front for some much more profitable business?" Otis asked me once when Madame Li seemed overly busy on the phone.

True or not, she was our friend, and often proved it. Today was no exception.

When Otis appeared from the kitchen, I thanked Madame Li and walked toward the woman sitting alone. Otis took my lead and arrived at her booth at the same time I did.

She was in her thirties, and I was certain she did not have sallow skin, dark circles beneath her eyes, and unattractive hair when she wasn't worried to death. She had hurriedly dressed or, more likely, hadn't cared what she'd thrown together when she pulled on a skirt and blouse that didn't come close to matching.

"Mrs. Bittmer?" Otis said. "Flora Bittmer?"

"Are you Otis Millett?"

"Yes, ma'am, and this is my partner, Kristin Van Dijk."

"How do you do, Mrs. Bittmer," I said. "We spoke on the phone yesterday."

"Yes. I recall. I'm trying to use my maiden name now. Graham. I divorced Carson Bittmer."

"We'll call you Flora Graham from now on," Otis said. "Come with us. Let's go upstairs to our office so we can have privacy."

She was like a sleepwalker, sandwiched between us, as we guided her up the back stairs and into our office.

"Judge Robbins recommended you," she said, when she was seated in one of our client chairs in front of Otis' big messy mahogany desk.

"Douglas Robbins?" Otis confirmed, as he settled into his desk chair.

"Yes. He's a friend of my father. Judge Robbins said no one would mess with you. Not even my ex-husband."

"He said that, did he? Well, I'm proud to hear of his recommendation. He is a fearless man of the law," Otis said and hiked a quizzical brow at me.

Flora clenched her hands and put her head down as if to cry.

"Here, here," Otis said and motioned to me.

I said, "May I get you something, Miss Graham? Something cool to drink, perhaps?"

"No, no, nothing. Just give me a minute."

We gave her the time she needed to regain her composure. Then, in a voice that was at first halting but grew stronger, she told the story of her difficult marriage to Carson Bittmer, co-owner of Bittmer Tooling.

The marriage was storybook because of the groom's business success and Flora Graham's historically famous family, with its four generations of Texas lore. All Texas school children can quote from the Bradshaw-Graham Treaty of 1894.

After the marriage, there were outbreaks of violence from time to time, but overall they were happy, until the occurrences of physical abuse began to happen closer together.

She would leave him and he would make promises, win her back, and be a good husband for a while before falling back into his violent ways.

No abused woman wants to hear her nightmare of a relationship is commonplace, but as stories of marriages and divorces went, Otis and I had heard this one before. It was the on again, off again aspect that made it a cliché.

Flora went on, "Fortunately there've been no children, though I wanted to start a family. But how could I trust him to be a good father when he couldn't be a good husband? The long hours and intensity of his work have created many of our problems, but that excuse can only go so far. So, after too many breakups and too many reconciliations, I have finally divorced him."

"You mentioned that Judge Robbins gave you our name," Otis said. "But what is he recommending that we do? Could you clear that up for me?"

"I have a court order issued by Judge Robbins that forbids Carson from coming near me."

"You told me about that. He'll be in contempt of court if he disobeys."

"The problem with that, Mister Millett, is Carson thinks rules and laws are for other people. He's said he'll come see me whenever he pleases. And he will, too. And when he does, he'll hurt me."

"I see," Otis said. "So, Judge Robbins thought I could talk with Mr. Bittmer maybe? Intimidate him? Remind him that disobeying a court order means police and jail time?"

An expression of disbelief crossed Flora's face.

"Talking won't do any good. He'd laugh at you," she said, her voice taking on an unpleasant edge. "The man sells oil field tools. He deals with nasty-tempered men every day of his life, tough men who have spent years at grueling jobs on oilrigs. Talk? No, I don't want you to talk to him. I want you to stop him from getting near me. I want you to break the man's neck if it comes to that to keep him away from me. Does that clear it up for you? Does that clear up what my daddy's longtime close friend the Honorable Judge Douglas Robbins thought you could do for me?"

Otis and I exchanged a concerned glance before he said, "Displeasing Judge Robbins ain't something I'm raring to do, but my agency will not agree to perpetrating grievous bodily harm. We can, however, agree to post an armed watch on your property with the understanding that the police are notified in writing from you that our purpose for being there is to uphold Judge Robbins' court order."

That took care of the basic arrangement. It was scheduling and terms after that.

When Flora Graham was ready to leave, she neither required nor desired an escort to her car, a late model chocolate brown Cadillac in need of a bath parked at the curb in front of the building.

I took an extra moment at the window to check the other cars on the street. No sign of our shooters.

"It turns out we're bodyguards, after all," I said when I turned back to the room.

Otis was making coffee. "Her daddy's good friend Judge Robbins is a vindictive, cantankerous old reprobate who would just as soon cancel our permit to do business as throttle his mother-in-law. No skin off his teeth. You tell me we were left any choice."

"You have some reputation, Otis."

"That old judge has run things his way for years, Missy. Respectable folks don't want to admit it, but it's dirty at the top, too. They just have better manners. I can't be bought and he knows it. But he likes to put the screws to me now and again to make sure I know the pecking order."

"But you're doing him a favor if you do this, aren't you?"

"I am for a fact, Missy. You're a smart gal."

I let the moment pass before I spoke again. "You want me to call the locksmith?"

"I'll take care of it. But ain't it strange as spooked as she was she wouldn't have changed her locks first thing?"

"People don't always know the practical things to do," I said. "Especially when they're scared."

Otis arranged for the locks, then spoke to a lieutenant he knew over at the Fort Worth Police HQ. He explained the situation, made it clear who was involved, and mentioned Judge Robbins' name twice. Once that was settled, he called B.K. Simmons, a retired cop he knew, to take the graveyard shift from 2:00 a.m. to 10:00 a.m. I was assigned 10:00 a.m. to 6:00 p.m. and Otis got the hot shift from 6:00 p.m. to 2:00 a.m.

Otis would start the job that day at six. I would relieve B.K. tomorrow morning, Sunday.

If Carson Bittmer were going to show up, the most likely time was after work when Otis was there, but in case he came later, half in the bag, the retired cop would be on duty. My shift was during normal business hours, the least likely time to have a confrontation with the hot-tempered Mister Bittmer.

Otis caught the phone when it rang.

He was brief.

When he hung up, he said, "That was Sidecar Sanchez. Spider Jack Tooley is our shooter's moniker."

"That mean anything to you?" I asked, my heartbeat quickening in spite of myself.

"It will. Sidecar asked about his books."

"*His* books? I haven't even talked to the store yet."

"They open on Saturday?"

"I think so."

"Why don't you go do that then while I do a rundown on Mister Tooley? When you see me next, I'll know what kind of scumbag we're dealing with."

18

I DIDN'T SPEAK. to Otis again until close to nine that evening.

I drove over to the snooty part of town, to the sprawling suburban ranch-style home where Flora Graham was hunkered down with her frazzled nerves and huge alimony. The black Olds 98 that Otis was driving was parked in the driveway near the house with him behind the wheel. I left my primered '50 Mercury at the curb and hiked up the long drive to join him.

There were lights on in the house. I didn't see any movement.

It was a pleasant evening; Otis had all his windows rolled down. He was laughing at something on the radio, but he had it at such a low volume, I was inside and the door was closed before I heard it was Spike Jones.

We listened and laughed together until the show was over.

"He always gets me going," Otis said.

I said, "Yeah, me, too. Listen, Wally closes at ten, so I need to move it along. I'm going to my place through the poolroom these days. I don't want to be in the alley after dark."

"That's smart, Missy."

It was the same reason Otis had a sawed-off shotgun in the seat next to him. It had nothing to do with Flora Graham and everything to do with the shooters who were gunning for us.

"What did you find out about Spider Jack Tooley?"

"He's a convicted felon, all right. Got a sheet the length of my leg. Mostly assault stuff. Armed robbery, too. I pestered the boys downtown to put out a warrant for his arrest. And I called Bull Smike, but didn't get aholt of him. Talked to that boy you was making eyes at."

"What boy would that be?"

"The one that put the whiskey in the trunk."

"You're a real busybody, you know that?"

"I think of myself as observant."

"You want to call Sidecar or do you want me to?"

"Get his books?"

"Uh huh."

"Nah, you tell 'im, now you've got such a special relationship with him."

"Where'd he get that moniker?"

"It's what he drinks. Some froufrou concoction that he can be persnickety about."

"Figures. I don't see him hanging on the side of a Harley."

"Call him Reggie to his face," Otis said. "Sidecar is for talking about him."

It was the next day that I met Sidecar in the Civic Auditorium parking lot. I got out and opened my trunk, and he walked over.

Sidecar didn't want to believe that at the price I was

talking about the books could be the ones he wanted. And then he removed his sunglasses and saw them snug in a box in the trunk of my car.

"You actually have them," he said.

"I paid for them. Why? You change your mind?"

"No, no. I'm just so delighted. Ten percent seems such a meager amount now, since you paid so little for them. I'm going to commission you twenty-five percent."

"Tell you what, Reggie. Reimburse me what I'm out and let's say I did you a favor. Okay? It's more friendly that way."

Reggie 'Sidecar' Sanchez fiddled with the chocolate brown kerchief peeking from the pocket of his impeccable pale green suit for a long moment before saying, "Would you be insulted if I bought you a pair of shoes?"

I suppressed a laugh, picked up the box of books, and said, "I'd be flattered. Open your door and I'll put these on your passenger seat."

It was as if an all-points bulletin had been printed in the daily papers. Spider Jack and Ugly disappeared. There were a lot of folks looking, but nobody was seeing them.

"That don't mean they ain't out there, Missy."

I agreed his warning was true and I was heeding it. But the days passed with no sign of the shooters and with Otis, B.K. Simmons and me just taking our shifts at Flora Graham's.

"Boring as bat shit, ain't it?" Otis had said to me the day before Carson Bittmer showed up near the end of my shift.

I knew who it was when a mud-splattered new Cadillac

slid to a stop at the curb in front of the house. A big guy about forty got out and came striding across the spacious lawn toward Flora's front door.

I was out of my car just as quickly and walking at an angle that would have me intercepting him before he got to the front porch.

He was a heavyweight with some serious upper body muscle. I was five-seven; he looked six-two. I was one-thirty; he looked two-twenty. I did not want the confrontation to get physical.

I spoke up while we were still several yards apart, but closing fast.

"Mister Bittmer. I'm here to remind you of the judge's order to stay away from your ex-wife."

He hurried his last couple of steps and was close to me sooner than I expected.

He tried to backhand me. I ducked and caught his arm, but he was too strong for me to handle.

He grabbed me by my hair and pulled me around so hard I thought my neck would snap. He jammed a hand between my thighs, picked me up by my crotch and the hair of my head, swooped me up shoulder high—and then I was falling, the sky and treetops were a blur. I understood what was happening only a split second before he slammed me to the grassy lawn on my back.

A Gorgeous George move.

I was stunned. Catching my breath took effort.

When I was able to roll over and lift my head, I saw Bittmer kick open the front door and enter the house.

It wasn't easy getting up. My spine felt seriously realigned, but at least nothing was broken.

I moved as fast as I could across the yard and porch and past the demolished door. As I entered, I heard a commotion back in the house and followed the signs of destruction and sounds of Bittmer shouting and Flora screaming.

I found them in the kitchen, on the tile floor.

Flora was on her back struggling, and Bittmer was straddling her. His hands, hidden from my view, were at her head.

My thought was he was strangling her.

I put some heat behind my swing and blackjacked Bittmer in the back of his head. He collapsed like a pole-axed steer, bleeding from where I'd struck him.

He was dead weight and hard to manage. I planted my feet, used my legs, and strained to pull him away.

When I dragged him from Flora, I discovered her choking. I pulled some paper from her mouth and she coughed and threatened to throw up.

"Here, Flora, sit up. Try to sit up."

Her voice was tremulous. "He tried to kill me." She began shaking and sobbing, "He tried to choke me."

Her face was damp with sweat, red and blotched, her nose was leaking a yellow mucous, her mouth was bruised and bleeding, her lips were raw.

"You're safe now," I told her, and got her to sit up.

I closed her flowered housecoat, under which she was naked, and tried to calm her. She continued to quiver and cry, holding her neck with both hands, and grabbing her breath in jagged gasps—until she saw Carson.

When she saw her ex-husband lying unconscious and bleeding on the floor near her, Flora Graham became concerned.

"You killed him," she cried out, no longer choking.

"I don't think so," I said, and leaned over to touch the artery in his neck.

Flora hit my arm with her fist and screamed, "Don't touch him. Don't touch him."

I got to my feet as she sprawled across her ex-husband shouting how much she loved him. That was all I needed.

I located the telephone, called the police, and went outside.

I got my black stocking cap from the car and put it on. I had learned that my platinum blonde hair caused men to take me less seriously than when I hid my hair beneath my cap.

Look at the way Carson Bittmer treated me, for example.

That caused me a private laugh—though I knew I would be reaching for the Ben-Gay tomorrow.

19

OTIS DROVE UP right on schedule. It was time for his shift to start.

He parked at the curb across the street and got out of his car just as the police arrived. Before we could meet mid-lawn, another police car arrived from the opposite direction. Moments later an ambulance arrived, followed by yet another police car.

"We ain't gonna have a lot of time. What happened?" Otis said as he walked up.

I told him the whole story in four or five sentences, so he was ready when the first patrolman trotted up to us.

Flora Graham came out holding up a woozy Carson Bittmer, who was pressing a folded dishtowel to his head. She cried out, "Arrest that woman. She attacked my husband."

The policeman said, "Is she talking about you?"

"She's confused," I said. "He attacked me."

"She destroyed my house," Flora Graham shouted.

Two patrolmen rushed across the lawn to meet with her.

"My lawyer is on his way here. I'm going to sue you," she screamed at me.

"Can she do that?" I asked Otis.

"Not likely," he said.

"She broke my door down," she shouted for her neighbors to hear. "I'm going to sue you," she told me again.

I gave Otis the paper that I'd removed from Flora's throat and he showed it to Sergeant Kelly, the officer in charge. It was the court order signed by Judge Robbins.

"You pulled this out of her throat?" the sergeant asked me.

"Yeah. Her ex-husband had stuffed it there," I told him. "She was choking on it."

"My husband tried to stop her," she shouted, "and she hit him. Look at his head. Look what she did."

According to Flora Graham, she was going to sue me for assault and breaking and entering and a list of other charges.

One of the policemen on the porch took a look at the size 12 footprint on the front door, and told Sergeant Kelly what he'd found. So, after hearing my story and using his car radio to confirm with Headquarters that we were acting within the law, Kelly directed his officers to arrest and put bracelets on Carson Bittmer.

Kelly said to me, "We'll need you to come downtown and answer some questions and fill out a report. Is that your car in the driveway?"

"Yes, sir. It is," I said and glanced at Otis, the real owner.

"That a forty-nine?"

"Fifty," I said.

He gave the car a once over.

"Nice condition. Getting ready to paint it?"

"Can't decide on a color."

"Always liked that model," he said. "My high school buddy John had a forty-nine. We used to double date, so I know the back seat better'n the front." He gave me a nice smile. "All right, we'll get this traffic cleared up so you can get out of here and follow us."

"I'll be happy to do that," I said, and rolled my eyes at Otis.

The drivers of the police cars and the ambulance performed the ballet that opened the street for traffic flow, and we were ready to go.

Otis gave me a nod and headed for the house to complete our business with the charming Miss Graham.

The Mercury was facing out, so when the patrol car carrying Carson Bittmer drove away, I was quickly behind it and we were on our way downtown.

I'm not certain what drew my eyes to the late model Dodge two-door that was parked up the street, but as I passed I saw Ugly behind the wheel and Spider Jack riding shotgun.

Christ!

They were scrunched down, but I saw them.

A quick thought was they'd followed Otis into the neighborhood and had gotten hemmed in by the emergency traffic that had arrived all at once.

I hit my brakes, slammed the reliable old Mercury into reverse, and was flying backwards in a flash with the tires screeching and smoking. I whipped into a turn with the intention of ramming the rear of my car into them.

However, Ugly—who without a doubt had the reflexes

of a twenty-year-old fighter pilot—had the tires of his car smoking at the same time and was peeling away as I was backing up. I barely missed the Dodge, and before I could stop my three thousand pound Detroit battering ram, it bounced over the curb and took out a fire hydrant.

I ground into low and fishtailed down the street bird-dogging the Dodge at about three car lengths, leaving a geyser of water behind me shooting forty feet in the air.

A patrol car that had pulled out to follow Sergeant Kelly and me slammed on its brakes, blocking the street. So, Ugly flew over the curb, tore through a tall hedge, and ripped across Flora Graham's exquisite lawn, scattering policemen and neighbors.

I had the pedal to the floor and followed Ugly and Spider Jack through the hedge, across Flora's lawn, through the flying pickets of a once charming fence, and into the front yard of the house next door. Ugly cranked a hard, sliding right turn on the neighbor's lawn, engine roaring, tires spinning, throwing sod and grass like a lawnmower turned backhoe gone berserk.

That maneuver cost the thugs time; I was catching up.

We careened back across the sidewalk and dived into the street doing forty and climbing, both of us clipping parked cars left and right. I saw the blinking lights of a police car whip in behind us.

Good.

Catching those two would only be the beginning. I'd caught them before. I knew what that was like. I welcomed the police coming along for the ride, as long as they didn't confuse me as being a criminal in this mess.

We were pushing sixty into the second block when

Ugly slammed on his brakes. I hit my brakes, too. His car and mine were sliding when he took a hard right up a drive, leaving me with a police car coming right at me.

The cops were on their radios; they were converging on the area.

I bullied my low-slung Mercury into a tight right to follow Ugly and avoid a head-on with the Fort Worth PD. When I got control, I realized that Ugly was driving across lawns and through hedges again, going back the way we'd come.

I took that turn, too, but this time Spider Jack's window was facing the street and he was shooting at the police car that had been following me. It was happening too fast for me to know if he was hitting anything, I just saw the flashes of his big cannon.

My car was whining at the top end of low gear as we ripped across lawns and through fences. I knew then that the only way to bring this to a finish was to ram my car into them. I could have done that on the street, but I'd reacted out of habit.

I shifted into second just as they came to a dead stop. The Dodge had hit a low stone wall and the rear end was rising up before my eyes.

Be careful what you wish for.

In a spine-jolting crunch that flattened me against the steering wheel, the Mercury slid under them and their car came down on my hood, leaving my horn blaring and my engine roaring.

I spun around in the seat, used both feet to push open the door, and moved fast. I jumped out, swung around the open door, and started forward with my pistol in my hand.

How did those felons get two houses ahead of me?

Spider Jack, a scarecrow with a stiff leg, and Ugly, a fat barrel on short, skinny legs, were making great time; they were almost to the cross street.

I waded through a jungle of calla lilies and followed them over the broken wall. I was a runner, not a commando. These yards were obstacle courses. I cut down to the sidewalk and put on the steam.

The killers were already in the cross street, stopping a car. I couldn't chance shooting at them. I kept running.

They dragged a woman driver from her car, threw her to the ground, and were peeling away by the time I ran into the street. I dropped to one knee, squeezed off a half dozen rounds at the stolen car's rear tire, and flattened it. It didn't stop them.

They kept going with the rim grinding sparks.

"Move. Move," I shouted to the woman whose car had been hijacked, and ran to help her up and out of the street as a patrol car, with its siren screaming, drifted around the corner and blasted past us. Another patrol car followed that one, siren wailing.

The police were seriously giving chase.

In the distance I heard more sirens approaching as I found a place at the curb for the shocked driver to sit down and gather her composure.

Sergeant Kelly's car drove up at a civilized pace and stopped across the street from me. He was riding shotgun.

He opened his door, stepped out, and spoke to me over the roof. "We have even more to talk about now, huh?" He gestured for me to come get in.

20

IT WAS LATE by the time Otis and I finished with the police investigation downtown, and he dropped me off at my apartment.

Lee had fallen asleep in the living room listening to Sinatra. I heated up and ate the take-out dinner he'd saved for me, and took a hot bath before I spoke to him.

He woke in an amorous mood and, to be honest, I found the concept appealing, except my back was killing me, thanks to Carson Bittmer and the Demolition Derby I'd lost. What might have been welcomed was restrained by a need for the warming application of Ben-Gay.

However, a similarity between applying a muscle relaxer and making love was being on the bed, naked. Lee, a sly and patient dog, used that to his advantage. And, the next thing I knew—

When I got to the office the next morning, though my spirits were flying, I still hadn't gotten the spring back in my step.

Otis noticed.

"You hurt from being thrown around by that Bittmer jerk?"

"Mmmm. Madame Li told me I should do Tai Chi with her in the mornings."

"Some kind of noodle dish?"

"It's an exercise you do slowly."

"A slow exercise?"

I nodded.

He gave me a critical face and changed the subject. "Spider Jack made a big mistake yesterday. He wounded a police officer and moved himself up to the top of the Most Wanted list."

I'd already heard they'd gotten away again. "He and that driver of his have nine lives," I said.

"Don't matter coon or cat, they all get treed sooner or later, Missy." He tapped a Lucky against the desk and lit up. "You feel good enough to take a drive with me?"

"What've you got?"

"Your very dear, very close friend, Sidecar Sanchez called."

"Oh, yeah?"

"Says he did some digging. Maybe knows where Spider Jack's holed up."

My heart jumped. "He gave you an address?"

"It's a maybe. He got it from Wrong Foot Reesler."

"He still on the sauce?"

"Reliability ain't his long suit, if that's where you're leanin', but sometimes even a drunk can see something."

"Where'd he see him?"

"A transient hotel."

The smell of the place was stale beer, mildewed carpet, and some foul indescribable something I didn't care to nail down.

It was an old two-story, wood frame affair with an out-of-order elevator. The tenants that were hanging around the grimy lobby weren't looking for work that day. Of those awake, none looked sober.

The only tenants who showed any signs of life were the tired mothers with small children making their way to and from the front door.

"Cheap housing," Otis commented when he saw the mothers and children. "Their husbands are looking for work or they're saving to find something better."

I hoped that was the explanation.

There was a teller's cage with a collection of wooden pigeonholes behind it, but no one was manning the desk. A manager's sign was on the door next to the cage.

Otis knocked.

We waited and were ready to knock again before a bleached blonde with split ends and dark roots finally opened up. She was five-four, maybe, wearing cutoff Levi's, a halter-top, and last night's eye makeup. She was young, but she didn't look healthy.

She had an unlit cigarette in her mouth.

"You the manager?" Otis asked.

It was a fair question. She could've been a high school truant.

"Wha'd'you want?"

"We're looking for someone we think lives here. Thought you might be able to help us."

From within, a man's voice said, "Who is it, Ruth Ann?"

"Mind your business," she said to him, and scratched a kitchen match across the face of the door and lit her cigarette.

"You cops?" she asked through the smoke.

"No, ma'am. We're not. We're doing some insurance investigation. There's been an accident and we're trying to locate one of the persons involved."

"Oh, yeah? One of the *persons*, huh?"

"Yes, ma'am, and we think he might be living here."

She looked at me and said, "Wha'd'you do?"

I said, "Excuse me?"

"You just along for the ride? Carry his briefcase? Like that?"

"No, ma'am," I said. "I'm an investigator, too. Do you think you might help us with our search for this person?"

She blew smoke at me.

"Why the hell would I do that?"

"To do the right thing…help find the party involved in the accident."

The manager worried with something in her mouth, something stuck between her teeth, and then said, "You know how many rooms I got here?"

It was a deep, narrow building. From what I could see past her, the rooms were small, the ceilings high.

"No, ma'am. A lot, I'd say."

"I'd say twenty-six. Twenty-six damn problems. Diapers in the johns. Drunks nose-divin' down the stairs." She took the cigarette from her mouth and snuffed it in a half-full glass of brownish liquid that sat on an end table near the door. "You know where my stupid husband is?"

"No, ma'am," I said.

"Doin' a nickel at Huntsville for toolin' around with

a chippy in a big Jew canoe that any nitwit could see didn't belong to 'im. The jerk left me with this dump or starve." She worried with her tooth again before saying, "You think I give a shit about who comes and goes here? Who forgets to report accidents? You really think I care?"

"I couldn't say, ma'am," I said. "But would you mind telling us if one of your twenty-six rooms is rented to a tall man with a big smile? A Gary Cooper-kind of looking man?"

"No name? You dancin' in the dark here, Towhead?"

"Actually, we do have his name, but we doubt he's using it."

She widened her eyes and waited.

"Tooley," I said. "Jack Tooley."

Guttural disgust was the best I could describe the sound she made. "You two morons are wastin' my time. Room twenty-three," she said, and slammed the door.

"A couple of times there I thought she was gonna bust into song," Otis said as we crossed the lobby to the street entrance.

Coming out onto the street, we were looking all directions. My hand itched to have a pistol in it. I couldn't speak for Otis, but I got a rush of adrenaline when I heard we had located where Spider Jack might be.

For all the obvious reasons, we didn't want to use the phone in the hotel lobby. Hell, I didn't even want to touch the phone, or anything else in that filthy place. So we walked across the street to a phone booth outside a café.

When Otis called downtown to get the police moving, I checked the time: 11:35.

When he hung up, I said, "We don't know if he's in there."

"And if he's gone, we don't know if he's ever coming back," Otis added. "But we're closer than we was. Let's go keep an eye on things until our backup arrives."

We started across the street.

Room twenty-three was on the second floor near the rear of the building, three apartments from the back stairs. There was an added flight of stairs that went up to the roof door that provided me a good position for watching the door to Spider Jack's room.

I pulled on my black stocking cap, stretched out near the top of that flight of stairs, and moved over against the back wall. No one coming up to the second floor or going down to the first could see me, but it gave me a clear view of the second story hallway and the door to room twenty-three.

Otis took up a position below me, around the corner where the hall jutted back to provide access to the roof stairs. He had to peek around the corner to see room twenty-three, so he was relying on my eyes.

All we had to do was keep watch until the police arrived. I was beginning to like the idea of the police arresting Spider Jack, and his driver, who we assumed was with him.

Lunchtime cooking odors were starting to compete with the natural stench of the place, and the bumps and squeals of restless children living in small spaces could be heard from the rooms down the hall.

Either the Fort Worth PD was taking forever, or time itself had decided to crawl.

The occasional mother herding her toddlers to the stairs was worrisome to me. I couldn't help but wonder what might happen if Spider Jack and Ugly came out and something got started with a family in the hall.

After thinking that, I saw a pregnant young woman making her way toward the stairs. She carried her handbag over her arm. She seemed weak. She was unsteady on her feet, and ran her hand along the wall as she moved toward Otis and me.

She paused here and there for long moments, her face distorted in pain. She passed room twenty-three and the next room before she cried out and, holding the wall, slipped to her knees and then collapsed to the floor on her back.

"Help me," she cried out. "Help me."

Her voice was desperate. When I was a teen, I'd seen a woman go into labor at a Woolworth's. The manager called her a taxi and one of the store clerks went with her to the hospital. I felt certain that was what was happening in the hallway below me. She was in labor and having contractions.

Otis took a look around the corner. She didn't see him, and he pulled back and glanced up at me.

"Help me," she called out again, after panting through a long contraction.

My heart was racing. Wasn't someone going to open a door and come out to help her? Call her a taxi? The sounds I had been hearing from the rooms down the hall were now silent.

Where were the police?

The next time she cried out, I wasn't surprised to see Otis step around the corner and go to her.

Dear Otis.

What did he think he was going to do? What could he do? She needed a doctor.

I could still see down the hall, but I saw more of Otis than the door to room twenty-three. I slid over, still lying on my side, uncomfortably stretched up the stairs, but I'd moved to the front edge to see better. I had a .38 in each hand to cover him.

He knelt, took off his jacket, and sat down at her feet with his back to the wall. They were talking, but with my hearing I wasn't getting much. I heard her say something about waiting. She couldn't wait, maybe. Otis was turned away from me, so I heard nothing of what he said.

I shouldn't have been surprised when Otis helped her take off her underwear. And yet, with all the signs, I wasn't prepared to think of Otis delivering a baby, much less in a hallway outside Spider Jack Tooley's room.

Where were the police?

They were trained for backseat births, weren't they?

I had a balcony seat and perfect eyesight. I saw the baby's head. My god, she was right about not being able to wait. Mama was crying and moaning with her head pushed forward, her teeth and fists clenched; baby wanted out.

I saw at once when the door to room twenty-three opened. "Otis," I said, and he looked past his straining patient to watch with me as Ugly and Spider Jack entered the hallway.

They saw a man and woman between them and the stairs, but didn't appear to grasp what was happening. Spider Jack was limping past them before he realized who Otis was, sitting on the floor wearing his fedora.

That put Ugly and Spider Jack between Otis and me

when they stopped and pulled their pistols. As they moved apart, I saw that Otis had his .45 in his fist, and that his patient was panting like a steam engine.

No time to waste, I called out, "Hey, Spider Jack."

His head snapped around, but he didn't see me, lying on the stairway up near the ceiling. He was confused and took a halting step or two away from Otis.

"Up here, Stupid."

He swung his pistol up toward me and was quick to see I had two pistols on him.

Better than that, sirens were arriving out front.

"Move along, Jack. It's not your day," I said.

He proffered his big toothy smile and kept his eyes on me. Ugly kept his eyes on Otis, and they sidled away with their pistols ready until they were out of my sight beneath the stairs.

Out of my sight!

My heart leaped. Adrenaline sent me sliding down the stairs feet first on my stomach as gunfire erupted.

Bullets tore through the wooden steps and risers where I had been. I fired back, both pistols jumping in my hands. I was punching lead blindly through the stairs, reaching out for those animals below me that were escaping down the stairs.

My ears were ringing and my heart was thundering as I hustled around to the head of the stairs to make certain Spider Jack and Ugly had taken off. Then I went to stand guard as Otis finished what he had started.

He was placing the newborn on its mother and covering it with his jacket as several policemen that had charged up the front stairs came running down the hall toward us.

The officer in front shouted, "We heard gunfire."

"They went down the back stairs," I told them and pointed.

Three patrolmen ran after Spider Jack and Ugly and one stayed with us. "She get shot?" he asked.

"Nah. She just had a baby. Come on," I said. "This is their room."

I kicked open the door to room twenty-three and entered with the policeman right beside me.

"I'm not sure that was a good idea," he said, looking at the splintered doorframe.

"It's an emergency," I said. "I need to call an ambulance."

"That's different," he said.

I picked up the receiver and dialed the operator as the policeman began snooping around Spider Jack's room.

21

THE MEDICAL ATTENDANTS who came to take Edna Foster to the hospital bragged on Otis. They asked him how he did this, how he did that, and seemed delighted with everything he did, especially when he covered the baby's ears during the shooting.

"The new mama screamed," Otis said, "but I told her to cover her ears, too.

"He's a natural," one of the medics said.

After the police gave us the okay, we walked the length of the hall and down the front stairs, talking all the way. I had never seen Otis so elated.

"I didn't do a thing," he said. "The little head came out and turned to the side and all I did was just guide her out and keep her from touching the floor. It's a little girl. Did you know that?"

"Yeah," I said. "You told me."

"A little girl. I was afraid about the cord, but the docs said I did right by just paying it no mind. They said they'd take care of it. Bears and dogs and things eat all that stuff. Did you know that?"

"I think I've read that, uh huh."

I was so proud of Otis.

"You know, Missy, I kept thinking about my dirty hands. The things I've done. And there my hands was holding that baby girl all innocent and new to this world. I don't never cry, but when I put that little girl on her mama, I felt like I might."

We crossed the vacant lobby, and stopped outside the front entrance.

Otis lit a cigarette.

I said, "One time my mother showed me a woman having a baby in a park. We were in Shawnee, visiting my grandma."

"When was that?"

"I was about six. So, nineteen forty-one or so, I guess. Mom pointed out an Indian woman under a tree. 'Do you see her?' she asked, and then knelt down beside me. I remember her face next to mine. She said, 'She's having a baby, Kristin.'"

"In the park?" Otis asked.

"Uh huh. I didn't know what it meant to *have* a baby. She was a distance from us, and I recall to this day what I saw. It wasn't much really, a longhaired woman on her back on a blanket. She looked like a bundle of clothing; her raised knees made kind of a tent of her long dress. After a while, I saw she had something in her hands. She wrapped it in a cloth, got up, gathered her blanket, and walked away. She was barefoot."

"I'll be," Otis said.

"I remember like it was yesterday, the way she left the park and walked off down the road."

"A strong Indian woman," he said. "Funny the things we remember."

"You'll never forget what happened here today."

"Reckon not." He laughed and shook his head. "It was a God wink miracle it all turned out okay. I must be blessed," he said.

Police Headquarters was taking the capture of Spider Jack Tooley seriously if the number of policemen walking to and from the hotel was any indication.

As Otis and I started across the street, I counted three cars had arrived to back us up—and then the bullets came at us.

The sound of gunfire was abstract, like an afterthought. However, the lead buzzing by at more than a thousand feet per second was as real as it gets.

None of it hit me, but my partner wasn't so lucky.

There was blood mist in the air. I saw him going down.

I pulled my .38, went to my knee, and searched for a target. There was a car roaring away. I wasn't certain. My head was swimming. Had the shots come from the car? It was already too far away. I fired low. I emptied a magazine at the back tires.

I heard other weapons firing. I heard shouting.

A police car whipped around, tires squealing, and gave chase to the fleeing car. I should've fired higher, sooner. I should've aimed for the driver.

"Otis. Otis," I heard myself saying as I rose looking for him.

He was crumpled in the street, blood everywhere.

"Get a doctor!" I shouted to the policemen running toward me. "Get an ambulance!"

I dropped to the asphalt beside my friend and began tearing at his clothing. He'd been hit several times. I had to stop the bleeding. I pulled a blade and cut away his vest and suit coat and shirt and tie. I pulled away the fabric to find his upper body wounds. He'd been shot three, no, four times, maybe.

A policeman ran up, breathing hard. Together we applied pressure at his wounds to stanch the bleeding. We both got covered in blood. Otis' blood.

"An ambulance is coming," the policeman said.

Through the pounding in my ears, I heard the siren. It was close.

Otis' voice sounded hollow. He said, "If the good Lord calls, I'm ready."

"Shut up with that," I told him.

"I know I ain't always been good…"

"Now you're making sense," I said.

"I'm falling, Missy. I'm falling…"

"Otis, look at me. Look at me. You're not falling."

A policeman was running toward us, waving his hands, shouting, "Over here, over here," and an ambulance attendant tugged at my shoulder, dragged me back, ordered me to let go and move aside.

It was difficult to find my balance, and I was the one who was falling and a policeman caught me and held me up.

"Where's he going?" I asked, loudly. "Where're they taking him?"

"Peter Smith Hospital," he said, gripping my arm. "Come on. I'll drive you."

22

OTIS WAS IN the emergency room at Peter Smith Hospital and no one was talking.

Lee had gone by the apartment and picked up a change of clothes for me. A nurse had taken my dirty clothes away.

"Our laundry knows how to get blood out," she'd said, and brought them back to me a few hours later, clean, ironed, and folded.

The doctors, nurses, and especially the policemen that came by were taking a moment and speaking to me. Those who knew Otis said nice things about him. The compliments were making me nervous.

"Is he going to die?" I asked the nurse who was being the nicest. "You can be truthful with me."

"He shouldn't, not with the doctors he has in there," she said, keeping her voice down. "But it's serious, and he's gonna be a while. Are you sure you don't wanna to go home and come back in the morning?"

It was late evening by then.

Lee had been called away to a crime scene.

Doc McGraw and Loretta had come by, but only stayed

a couple of hours. They had a sick foal they were watching. Doc assured me that Otis was under the care of the best in the business.

Henry sat with his head in his hands, unable to sustain a conversation. He was pale and introspective while he was there, and reluctant to leave when it was time to go.

He seemed ashamed that commerce should dictate his schedule, but he was running a man short on his crew and they had a counter and window installation at a savings and loan in Weatherford.

He promised to come back after work the next day.

Madame Li made a late appearance with several dozen gladiolas. Two of her waiters accompanied her carrying baskets of food for those who were standing vigil. Unfortunately, I was alone at that point, and I wasn't hungry.

Word got around, though, and it was nice to see the nurses and a doctor or two enjoy a break from the cafeteria food.

After Madame Li left, I stayed a bit longer, but the nurse was right. I wasn't going to be let in where they were tending to Otis, and he wasn't coming out to see me. What was I doing?

It was well after midnight when I walked out of the hospital. I felt lost.

I didn't know where I was going until I got into the taxi. I wasn't ready for home yet, so I decided to drop by the office. I hadn't been there since morning, and checking with our answering service would be something to do.

Anything to do, while I avoided thinking about life without Otis.

What I *was* thinking about during the taxi trip was why we hadn't been alert coming out of the hotel. All the baby talk, maybe. Or, more likely, the cops all over the place. Who would've figured those bastards for an attack in front of a half dozen cops?

They got away again, of course, because Ugly could drive at the Indy 500 and win. That and Spider Jack's arrogance made me think they were only going to become more daring with their attacks.

But why take such chances to kill us? The mercenary answer was they were pros and Travis Horner was paying them well for the job.

But why is Travis Horner so intent on killing us? There's no doubt in my mind that he's been behind the efforts to kill Otis. I'd become a target, too, but only because of Otis. He'd been targeted for death from the beginning.

Again, why?

If it was something to do with his past life, when he and Dixie were on the outs and he was drinking, Otis doesn't seem to know what that was. Or, he's not ready to say. More recently, he bashed Travis Horner in the face and broke his foot and Horner carries a mean grudge.

That's simple enough.

Travis Horner's a spoiled man with a big ego. His girlfriend runs away. His plan to get her back and punish those who helped her falls apart. Otis was supposed to have been punished for reasons known only to Horner, but instead Otis and I punish Horner and his minions.

Horner snaps and insists that Spider Jack finish the job he was paid to do, kill Otis. And then, like Henry says, bring back the girl and the thing.

"You sure this is where you want out?" the taxi driver said as he pulled up to the curb around the corner and down the street from our office building. "I don't know of any apartments around here."

"This is perfect. Thanks."

I paid and tipped him, got out, stepped across the sidewalk into the shadows, and paused. He didn't move.

"Got a problem?" I asked him.

"You okay? This ain't the best neighborhood. No businesses open for blocks."

"I'll be fine. Please go ahead."

He didn't look happy about it, but he said, "Whatever you say, sister."

I let him drive away before I thumbed the thin strap over my head to secure my handbag, and pulled on my black stocking cap.

After all my mulling it over in the taxi, I still wasn't certain why Horner was gunning for Otis and me, but I was sure about one thing, no more mistakes. I was going to stay alive through vigilance.

Alongside the building where he dropped me off, there was a narrow driveway that led to the far back corner of the parking lot behind our building. There were no lights in the lot and no lights on in any of the buildings that backed up to the lot.

I stopped in the shadows at the end of the driveway and enjoyed the soft, warm breeze that moved between the buildings as I loaded my pistols with fresh magazines from my handbag.

I watched everywhere as I moved around the back edge of the dirt and gravel parking lot with a pistol in my hand. I didn't rush. I was dressed in black, there wasn't much of a moon, and I kept to the shadows. If there was an assassin in the lot, I was determined to see him before he saw me.

The only cars that stayed the night in the lot were in the back corner, three rust buckets that belonged to our agency. We used them on stakeouts. They had good tires, smooth-running powerful engines, and looked like junkers. I planned to drive one home later.

It was approaching 2:00 a.m. by the time I let myself in the back door of the Mandarin Palace. Palace Guard, the mouse catcher that patrolled the premises at night, knew I had entered and wandered over with her tail high to say hello, but no human would've heard me.

The same with the backstairs. I knew them intimately and could ascend or descend without a squeak. Otis was a horse of a different clunk. He sounded like an army going up or coming down.

"I want 'em to know I'm comin'," he told me.

When I opened the door at the top of the stairs and entered the upstairs hall, I knew something was wrong. When our old floor fan was on, which was normally 24 hours a day, it created a hum that the floor carried. I didn't notice it when it was on, but missed it when it was off.

It was off.

23

I COULD HEAR snoring through our office door.

I still had my pistol in my hand.

Without a sound, I turned the knob and opened the door a crack. The streetlight from the window showed me a man on the sofa, seated with his head back, asleep and snoring. His pistol, something small, was placed on the coffee table in front of him.

Another Einstein, Otis would've said.

But I didn't want to jump to conclusions. This guy could be a cop sent over by a friend of Otis' to watch out for me.

I entered the office, listening for sounds from the other room. I didn't hear anything.

I moved to the coffee table, picked up his little pistol and had a look at the guy. He was just a kid, too young to be a cop in plain clothes. The pistol was wrong, too. Cops in Fort Worth didn't carry Berettas.

I had a thug to report to the police for breaking and entering.

I stuffed his peashooter in my hip pocket, then reached over and tapped his knee with the tip of my pistol barrel.

That woke him up.

He was confused.

He focused on me, standing in front of him, slapped his hand on the table searching for his pistol, but couldn't find it. He panicked, grunted a high-pitched moan, and froze, his eyes wide and staring.

I heard the thump of feet hitting the floor. Someone had gotten off the bed in Otis' apartment.

Keeping the kid covered, I moved around the end of the coffee table so I could watch the door into the next room. When I glanced away, the kid made a mistake. He reached down and came up with a revolver from his ankle holster.

I put two in his chest, and then gave my full attention to the other room.

There was a pause before heavy footsteps in the other room made for the hall door. The man kicked open the door, raced down the hall, and down the front stairs. I heard the downstairs door slam shut.

I stepped over and looked out the window, but by that time there was nothing to see on the street.

I left the lights out and, using caution, entered Otis' apartment. Streetlight from the windows showed the room undisturbed, save the damaged door. I went over and pulled at the splintered wood, but it was too badly smashed to close.

When I turned back into the room, I caught a punch high to my jaw that knocked me to the floor. I was dizzy for a moment, but had enough of my wits to bring up my weapon, which I still held in my hand.

"I'll take that," the large man said, and damn near broke my arm yanking my piece from my grip.

He tossed it across the room to clatter on the floor.

"Thought you scared me off, didja little mama?" he said.

I rolled over and started up, but he grabbed me from behind. He was big enough to lift me off my feet and into his arms. I twisted around to face him as he pulled me closer to his chest.

"You're gonna wish I'd run off," he said, his foul cigarette breath hot against my face.

I began kicking and kneeing him, but he smiled and squeezed me tighter. So I head butted him in the face.

He reared back and let me go, as blood burst from his nose down the front of his shirt and all over me.

Instead of falling away from him when he released me, I clutched his shirt with one hand and snatched his revolver from his shoulder holster and swung it up toward his face. He grabbed the weapon just as I let one go into the ceiling.

Jesus!

A fired round inside a room is loud enough, but when the pistol is a Smith 357 right next to your face it's like needles jammed in your ears. He and I both cried out, and I let go.

I landed awkwardly and totally deaf.

Before I could get my balance, he gripped my shirt with one hand and swung me into the wall, a lath and plaster wall that didn't give. I hit with my body, not my head, but the impact stunned me nevertheless.

My ears were throbbing a fuzzy silence. They were painfully attempting to return to normal as I struggled to get to my feet. I never took my eyes from him.

Blood was still pouring from his nose as he holstered his pistol.

He holstered his pistol instead of shooting me. Why?

I went for my other .38, but he snatched me up with both hands, and slammed me into the wall again. I protected my head a second time, but how long was I going to be able to do that? I fell to the side, sliding down the wall to the floor.

I saw the kick coming, twisted to avoid it, and was already crawling away when his boot hit the wall. I crabbed away fast on my hands and toes, but he caught me by my ankle, dragged me to him, and punched me in the back of my head.

Holy Shit!

He didn't knock me out, but he sure knocked me silly.

My ears were clanging; my head was spinning.

By the time I had my brains unscrambled, he'd found the Beretta in my pocket and my other .38 and pitched them aside and pulled up my pants leg, gotten my .32 from my ankle holster, and thrown it the length of the room.

"Did I get 'em all? Want me to keep lookin'?" He ran his hand up the leg of my jeans.

I kicked at him, pushed away, took a rolling tumble, scrambled to my feet, and turned to face him. I was dizzy, but I tried not to show it as I stumbled backward.

I was trying to get into the other room, but ended up on the far side of Otis' bed, between the two windows. Light from the street colored the guy's skin dusty yellow and the blood all over his face shiny black.

He smacked an ear with the palm of his hand and shook his head, flinging blood around him. "My ears are still ringin', you little fucker."

Blood flowed over his mouth and dripped off his chin, as if he needed to appear more fearsome. He moved around the end of the bed, snuffling for air through his damaged nose. "We ain't finished, little mama."

The choppy steps forward and the way he brought his fists up told me he had done some boxing.

I blocked a jab, collapsed to my haunches, and felt the breeze of a roundhouse right fly by me. I didn't want him to hit me again. I threw an arm up over my face.

He reached down, got me by my shirt collar, and dragged me to my feet. Before I could do anything, he had me by my belt, and pitched me like a rag doll across the bed to tumble over the coffee table there and onto the floor.

The big guy came around the end of the bed, snuffling for air. "We're gonna see how much you can take. Think you're so tough."

He was going to beat me to death because he liked what he was doing. That's why he didn't shoot me.

I couldn't let him get his hands on me again.

As I got to my feet, I turned so he didn't see it happen, and pulled a blade from my boot. Keeping my knife hand behind my leg, I used my foot to push the coffee table toward him as he came at me.

He easily stopped it, snatched the solid piece with both hands, swung it up, and let it fly across the room.

I stepped in fast and was next to him the instant he released the table.

His hands were above his head when I drove the knife hard up under his ribs. If he hadn't been so thick in the middle, it would've stuck out his other side.

He brought his arms down before I could stick him again and pushed me away. My bloody hand slipped from the handle, and the blade stayed in him.

He didn't even look bothered.

He pulled his lips back, clinched his teeth like a pit bull, and tore the knife from his chest.

It was a grand gesture that threw a rope of warm blood across my neck and shoulders and left him holding the dripping knife at arm's length.

"I'm gonna cut your tongue out."

I believed him.

My ribcage was having a hard time containing my heart as I backpedaled, never taking my eyes from the maniac who wanted me dead.

The doors were on the other sides of the room; I was retreating toward a wall with nowhere to go. I shot a glance toward our darkroom and beyond that was the bathroom, but those places wouldn't do me any good, even if I could get to them without him catching me.

I would drop down and kick at him, anything to keep the blade away from my upper body.

He shuffled another step toward me and stopped.

His face drooped.

He swayed.

He put out a hand to catch his balance. There was nothing to grab but me. I shoved his arm aside.

He turned away, but kept his gaze on me until his eyes glazed over and his mouth gaped open. He shuffled one more step and dropped the knife as his legs gave way. His head fell forward, then swung to the side, and uttering a long sigh, he sank to the floor.

I stayed where I was, leaning against the wall, catching my breath, willing my heart to slow down, wishing my head would quit throbbing.

After a long moment, I knelt down, yanked out his shirttail, and cleaned my knife on it. He would've died from the stab wound in any event, but if he'd left the blade in place, instead of pulling it out like Burt Lancaster, he would've had the time to kill me.

Violence requires a cold and deadly style, Wilde said.

I found my .38's on the floor near the bed. I liked the feeling of them in my hands. My .32 was over by the armoire. It looked clean enough to go back into my ankle holster. I didn't see the Beretta. I'd let the police find that.

I took off my purse and examined the stains. It was suede, new, and ruined. I didn't know why I ever thought I could have anything nice.

To give my heart time to calm down, I went into the bathroom and washed the blood from my hands and face. It was too soon to change my blood-slick clothing.

I gazed in the mirror and spoke to my image.

"Was it Spider Jack or these screw-ups who shot Otis?"

I was angry. I wanted screaming, rampaging revenge. But, as Wilde would suggest and as all my teachers instructed me, I held my fury at bay.

I breathed deeply and calmed down as I used a damp cloth to clean my pistols before I holstered them.

Careful not to walk in the blood pooling around the tough guy, I bent over him, took the .357 from beneath his arm, and checked the load. One fired, five ready to go.

I went into the office and had a look at the kid on the sofa. He hadn't moved since I'd last seen him. Another promising underworld career cut short.

I headed into the hallway with the cocked .357 in my hand. Maybe there were men waiting downstairs. More men hired by Travis Horner to kill Otis and me. Or, maybe not, but I was going to find out.

I didn't see anyone in back when I came in. And if

they were in front, I felt pretty sure they didn't know about a stairway that came up from the kitchen to the restaurant storeroom.

I used caution anyway as I went down those stairs, out the back way, and around to the side of the restaurant.

I stopped in the shadows near the corner of the building and remained motionless as I watched the cars that were parked along the street.

Angels of Death don't hurry.

I saw movement.

The four-door Lincoln.

Keeping to the shadows, I got to where I could see there was only one man in the big car, the driver. I figured the plan was to murder me, then drive to an after-hours place, have beers and a laugh, and count their easy money.

He turned his head.

The streetlight gave me his face.

He was Mexican, a middle-aged guy.

Holding the heavy pistol beside my leg, I moved without sound. I was next to his open window for several seconds before he became aware of me standing there, slightly behind him. He had to turn his head and peer over his shoulder to look into my eyes.

Under his breath, he said, *"La malandrina."*

"I'm not a bad girl," I said. "You're a bad man."

His bullet burst through the door to my left. I felt the shock and heat of it as it passed, spraying slivers of hot metal and powdered glass.

I began firing as I brought the powerful .357 up, stitching holes through the door and into the shuddering driver, starting at his hip, one above the other until the last bullet caught him in the neck just below his jaw, and the hammer was falling on spent brass.

Well, maybe I hadn't held *all* my fury at bay.

I tossed the empty revolver into the car with the dead guy and walked away.

24

I COULDN'T TAKE another police inquiry. My body ached, every muscle, every joint. I wanted to go where it was quiet and safe, shower away the blood, and sleep in my own bed. The bodies I was leaving behind weren't going anywhere.

On the way home, I stopped at a filling station phone booth to call Madame Li. I felt she was owed an explanation. Sometimes tenants throw around beer bottles and make noise, but what she was going to find in the morning was extreme by anyone's standards.

"Two men broke into our office tonight, Madame, and set a trap for me."

"Did they hurt you?"

"No," I said.

"Thank the gods," she said.

"They meant to kill me, but I killed them."

"Oh, my."

"These may have been the men who shot Otis."

"How will you ever know?"

"Ballistics, maybe."

"What is that?"

"Bullet comparison."

"I am proud of you," she said. "How was Otis when you left the hospital?"

"The same. Holding his own."

"I want him back upstairs good as new."

"Madame..."

"Yes?"

"Please call the police in the morning when you discover the bodies."

"I shall."

"And don't touch anything. Doing that will only create problems for you."

"Of course," she said.

"The Millett Agency will stand good for the damages."

"Damages are of no concern to me, Miss Van Dijk."

I remembered the driver.

"They'll find another man in a car parked out front."

"I see."

"And when the police arrive..."

"Yes?"

"Feel free to tell them you think I'm at the hospital where Otis is recovering."

"Who's the driver?" Lee asked me early the next morning.

"The driver? What are you talking about?"

I was still in bed. He was standing at the chiffonier, putting on his tie. I had a headache from hell.

"You were talking in your sleep."

That caught my attention.

"I do that? Talk in my sleep?"

"You did last night. You said the driver was a family man."

The driver was as bad as the others, but his death was going to stick with me. I never knew why some did. Maybe because he called me a bad girl.

I sat up.

Someone was hammering on my head.

I swung my feet over the edge of the bed, shook out some aspirin tablets from the bottle I kept on the bedside table, and reached for the glass of water.

"I wouldn't take those," Lee said.

"Why's that?"

"You haven't seen your face."

I put my hand to the left side of my head where the tough guy sucker-punched me. It hurt from my ear to my eye.

Lee was watching me.

I got up and took a moment catching my balance. It was as if I had a flat tire as I limped to the mirror. I had a shiner, all right, mostly black, but it would turn green and yellow over the next day or so if I didn't do something about it.

Lee was right. Aspirin would've thinned my blood and made the bruising worse. Doc McGraw had taught me that.

"I'd better ice this down."

Lee followed me to the kitchen and poured me a cup of coffee while I made an ice pack with cubes and a dish-towel.

"So who's the driver?"

I said, "The driver? Just a dream, I guess."

"You have things soaking in the bathroom."

"I'm sorry. Are they in your way?"

"Not at all, but I thought Peter Smith cleaned your clothes for you."

"They did. The things in there are from later, after I left the hospital."

"So your black eye didn't happen when you and Otis were attacked?"

"No, later," I said.

I sat down at the table and put the ice pack on my face.

"You got blood on your new purse?"

"Yeah, 'fraid so."

Lee sat across from me. "You're going to tell me about this, right?"

"It may have been the same guys who shot Otis," I told him. "They were waiting for me at the office."

"An ambush?"

"That's what they had in mind."

"And?"

"I killed them."

"Two men?"

"Three," I said.

Lee's brow wrinkled and his breathing changed as he took a moment to adjust.

"You killed three men?"

I assumed the question was rhetorical, since I had just told him I had.

He seemed distracted as he went on, "You want to talk about this?"

"You mean to you? Talk to you?"

"Well, yeah, me. But maybe a professional, too. You've had a couple of hard days. Maybe some time off, some time away would be a good idea."

"You probably mean well, Lee..."

He got up. He seemed too nervous to stay seated.

"I know. I know. I probably shouldn't've said that. Look, here's the problem: this could sound like a vendetta. Otis gets shot in front of half the Fort Worth PD and now his partner knocks off three hoods. Spider Jack wasn't one..."

"Of the men last night?" I finished for him. "No such luck."

There was a long pause. We both had some coffee.

Finally, Lee said, "Did you see what the newspapers did with your car chase?"

"Haven't had much reading time," I said.

"You know the stuff. Why aren't the police taking action? Even our better neighborhoods aren't safe. Look, sweetheart, things are getting touchy downtown. Tell me what happened, so I can tell you what to watch out for. Because even if you don't want to talk about it, the police are going to insist."

I told Lee a complete, though abbreviated version, from the time I went up the back stairs until I drove off to come home. I left out phoning Madame Li.

He said, "You should call downtown, let them in on what happened, and where they can find you. It's still early. You're in for some grief for not calling last night, but doing what I'm suggesting this morning will help you."

"You're right," I said. "I'll do it."

"And, Kristin...?"

"Yeah?"

"I know you'll wear dark glasses for a few days, but a black eye will support your story with the boys downtown. And..."

"Yeah?"

"Play to the hilt the helpless gal who got lucky. It'll be easier for them to accept."

"Mmmm," I said.

"And do something for me, will you?"

"Sure. What?"

"Think about talking with someone. Will you?"

"I'll think about it."

"And be extra careful until we collar this Spider Jack guy. Okay? We'll get him, but until we do, extra careful. Okay?"

"Okay," I said, and gave him a brave smile. Just a helpless little girl trying her luck.

It worked.

I got a gentle kiss on my cold black eye, and in parting, he said, "Sorry about your new purse."

25

"YOU GONNA SNOOZE the day away?"

But Otis didn't hear me.

He was all wires and tubes, and his bed was semi-circled with stainless steel machines with dials and gauges, machines that hummed and beeped. His doctor assured me that the emergency room at Peter Smith was as up to date as any such facility in the country.

"Ahead of most," he'd added.

I was happy to hear that because Otis was alive, and I hadn't been at all certain he would be when they brought him in yesterday. The doctors weren't sharing any details, but I knew Doc McGraw would find out and tell me. He had friends at the hospital.

The head nurse showed concern for my bruised face and gave the eye itself a close look. When I told her I was fine and was using an ice pack, she gave me some pills for pain and then dropped the subject. She'd seen worse. She told me if I remained in the chair beside the bed and didn't touch anything, I could stay for a while.

If my partner had been awake, he wouldn't've put up with all the modern medicine they had stuck in him and hung on him. He would've asked me to get the alum and pliers, and between us, we'd've taken care of it.

I laughed aloud about that and looked around the room. I seemed to remember small sad houses all in a row without the benefit of trees and men watering bedraggled lawns, men gone stale in midlife, having given up, flattened out, just standing around waiting for orders from their wives.

"That will never be Otis," I said.

I was glad we were alone. The pain pills had made me loopy.

I said to him, "You and Henry are my only family. You know that, don't you?"

I'd told myself no crying, and I had to look away for a few moments to keep my word. "Only you and..." I said, before allowing my gaze to drift back to my friend. "Okay, it's not about me. Just don't start thinking the rodeo's over, because it's not."

We had a few minutes of silence together, something Otis and I were never afraid of. Then a nurse came in. She squeaked around the room in her rubber soles, hovering over her patient and his monitors. She was making notes on his chart when the head nurse joined us.

"The police are looking for you," she said.

After I said hello to some familiar faces, and we had gotten past the fact that I was making a habit of coming to the station to discuss my involvement in all the newsworthy events happening in the city, I was seated in the metal chair at the metal table once again.

I told the truth. So, when I repeated the story for the lead detective on the case, it came out the same. Oh, little stuff got added or moved a tad as I remembered this or that, but what I told him was what had happened. And still, he wasn't happy with it.

Then it dawned on me.

He wasn't looking for the truth.

What was keeping me in that shiny painted interrogation room where everyone's voice rang hollow against the bare walls was the fact that a *girl* had killed three armed gangsters. Shots had been fired, a fight had occurred between a *girl* and a much bigger man, a knife had been used, and the *girl* came out tattered at the edges, but the winner.

It was hard for him to swallow, so this square-jawed veteran with the graying crew cut kept chewing on it.

I remembered what Lee told me and said, "I got lucky. Is that what you want to hear?"

"Do you think I want to hear that?" the lead detective named Lynch said, his cheeks getting red again.

"You know Otis Millett, right?" I asked, keeping my voice low and calm.

"I think you know I do. So?"

"So, I'm Otis Millett's partner. You think I'm a pantywaist?" He didn't know what to say to that. "I'll put it another way. You want to ask Otis if he has a pantywaist for a partner?"

"Okay, make your point," Lynch said.

"Two of the scumbags were easy and the other one damned near killed me before I killed him. What more of a point is there? If what happened last night wasn't self-defense, what is?"

"I don't doubt what happened was self-defense. Who said it wasn't? No one here denies that."

"What then? I described the fight to you in detail...

twice. The big guy landed the best punches, but I landed the last one. End of story."

The veteran leaned across the table, kept his voice conspiratorial.

"You know what keeps it from being the end of the story, Otis' partner? Two things. That knife is one." He paused and stared at me and tapped the table with his forefinger.

Patience has its limits, and he was testing mine.

Finally, he said, "What're you doing with a knife like that? That's a military knife, a killing knife. Commandos carry that knife. Where'd you say you got it?"

"From my boot."

"Don't be smart. Where'd you get the knife?"

"Originally, you mean. It was given to me by a commando who taught me to use it."

Lynch sighed and tapped the table some more before saying, "And two...I've been at this job for as many years as you've been alive. I've questioned a long list of people involved in shootings, including females. Not so many, but some. Okay? And you don't fit the pattern, miss. According to you, you killed three thugs who were trying to kill you. Have I got that straight?"

"That's what happened."

"You shot the boy on the sofa who pulled an ankle piece."

"Yes."

"You were surprised by a man who, even though you'd shot his pal and he'd gotten the drop on you, chose not to shoot you, but to throw you around and beat on you until you finally knifed him in the heart."

"I found that odd myself, but that's what happened."

"And then you went downstairs and confronted the third man who was waiting in the car. He shot at you and missed. You shot him multiple times and killed him. Right?"

"That's the short version, but it works," I said.

"See? You make light of it. That's what's wrong here. In all these years, the females I've spoken to who were involved in violent acts that threatened their lives were basket cases, during and after. They didn't enter rooms at 2:00 a.m. to confront a thug with a pistol or fight a man who was trying to beat them to death or, watch this one, after two killings, go downstairs and start it up with a man with a gun. Not one of them carried the fight to her attacker. Well, that's not exactly true. One wife stabbed her husband so many times we quit counting. She's still crocheting booties somewhere. But you get my point."

My mother used to say that it was better to keep my mouth shut and be thought a fool than to open it and relieve all doubt. I said nothing.

Lieutenant Lynch went on, "Knowing you were coming in, I read the report on the attempted armed robbery and shooting at Wally's Lunch Room. I agreed the shooting was justified, but I had to think, too, how quick you were to pull that trigger. What would've been wrong with keeping him covered till we arrived? And the perp said you kicked him, too. Twice."

I said, "To be fair, Lieutenant Lynch, I was looking down the business end of that guy's weapon before I shot and kicked him. He had my nerves on edge."

"I know. I know. I said it was justified; it's just that, well, I think you're too casual with all this gunplay. If you were a stone killer on your way to the chair, okay.

But you're not. On your way in I heard you laughing with Kelly about the car chase. He likes you, talks about how nice you are. You date a Dallas detective. You work with Otis Millett sneaking up on philandering housewives at local motels. But to hear you tell about last night you'd think you went around shooting folks all the time, and that's not true, is it?"

I smiled. "It really sounded like that?"

"I'm afraid so. It worries me that you killed three men, went home, had a good night's sleep, and gave us a call the next day. You see where I am with this, Miss Van Dijk? I'm wondering if you don't need to talk to someone."

That was twice today I'd gotten that advice.

I said, "I appreciate your concern. I think what happened last night fell too closely behind Otis being put in the hospital. I remember wondering if those were the same guys who'd shot him. Maybe I wouldn't have acted so brashly if I hadn't just come from being with my partner who's in the hospital hooked up like some lab experiment."

"Maybe. Maybe. And you were shot at yourself, weren't you? I mean when Otis got hit."

"Mmmm," I replied, remembering the buzz of the passing lead.

"And you're sure you don't know your assailants from last night?"

"Never saw them before."

"Why would they want to kill you? Why would some out of town heavies want to kill you?"

A brief discourse on Travis Horner's wily ways would have fit nicely there, but I decided against opening that can of worms.

I said, "Finish what they started with Otis, maybe?"

"Friends of Spider Jack Tooley?"

"That's what I'm thinking," I said.

"But, in fact, you don't know."

"Mmmm."

"When Otis is better, I want to discuss Jack Tooley with him."

I pushed my chair back and stood up. "I can't think of anything to add. If you don't mind, I'd like to go back to the hospital."

He also pushed his chair back and stood up.

"There'll be a formal inquiry. Stay available."

I nodded my agreement.

"I want to say thank you for your help, Miss Van Dijk, but I keep thinking it's too soon for thanks. There are things about all this that just don't feel right yet."

"One more thing," I said.

He stared at me.

"When the ballistics come back I'd like to know if those were the guys who shot my partner."

He continued to stare at me.

"Because if they're the same guys, Otis'll be proud of me...since I will have solved a case for you guys."

I put on my dark glasses and felt Lieutenant Lynch's eyes on me as I walked out.

26

THE HEAD NURSE in Intensive Care told me the wiry little guy in the overalls and plaid shirt had been in the waiting room most of the day. He wasn't much older than I and looked like a guy who worked construction, with his high-top tan work shoes and sunburn.

"He asked about Otis," the nurse said. "I thought you should know."

I went over and introduced myself; he got to his feet, pushing his thick brown hair from his forehead.

"Cooty Foster," he said, and gave me a big smile.

"I'm sorry, should I know you?"

"I reckon not. Edna's my wife. Your partner delivered our girl."

"Well," I said, and stuck out my hand. "Congratulations."

"Thank you, ma'am," he said and we shook. He had the calluses of a man who worked with his hands.

"How're your wife and daughter doing?"

"Purty good, I'd say. Another day here might could help, but we barely got through this part what with me jest catchin' odd jobs."

"Where're you from?"

"We was over near Little Rock. Went there fer some work, but it run out and Edna wanted to come home fer birthin' the baby. She's a Texan through and through."

"So you're from Arkansas?"

"You're askin' where'd I come up?"

I smiled. "I guess I am."

"Missouri born, and up and down the Mississippi after that," he said. "I don't mean to be puttin' my nose where it don't belong, ma'am, but was it the ruckus yesterday got your eye lookin' like that?"

"Something different," I said.

He pulled a concerned face. "But kin to yesterday, I'll bet."

"I'll be fine. It was nice of you to drop by. Otis is still sleeping…"

"He's gonna wake up, ain't he? Me and Edna's worried about him."

"He'd better snap out of it if he wants to stay on my good side," I said.

"We tried to come up with somethin' outta Otis, but couldn't make nothin' nice from it. So we're callin' our girl Millie after Millett. You like it?"

I was surprised and delighted. "I do like it. And I know Otis will, too." And then I thought of something. "What kind of work do you do, Mister Foster?"

"Call me Cooty or Bobby Lee if you have to, but mister don't fit me."

"Okay, Cooty. What're your skills?"

"I'm a carpenter by trade. Well, I been a carpenter's apprentice fer durn near six months, but I'd do pert near anything right now."

"You have a car?"

He let out a snort and pushed his hair back. "A half ton on its last legs is what I got."

"Will it get you to Weatherford?"

"Over west of here? That Weatherford?" I nodded. "Yes, ma'am, I guess it will. What's over there?"

"A job," I said.

I rustled up a scrap of paper, wrote a note to Henry, and gave it to Cooty with instructions how to find the savings and loan. Then I spoke to a nurse and told her the Millett Agency would guarantee the bill and to allow Edna Foster to stay in her room.

I knew Otis would approve.

Cooty Foster ran from the hospital to get on his way to Weatherford. I just hoped he knew one end of a hammer from the other. But something told me he did.

Bull Smike left a message with our service. I called him back and told him briefly what had happened to Otis. He was in town and came right over to the hospital.

I was glad to see him, though I wasn't certain why. Maybe, in some strange way, it was because I had met so much of his family.

I half expected him and his sons to come striding through the hospital corridors with their shotguns at ready. But Bull Smike was alone, dressed in his Sunday best, and approached me with his hands extended to take both my hands in sympathy.

I'd seen my mother's friends do that to Aunt Dora at my mother's funeral. I wondered if he was exporting an Oklahoma custom.

Holding my hands, he leaned toward me with his head canted, his good eye wide and intense, and said, "You tell me if you need anything. Anything. I owe you and your partner, and I won't have you want for a thing at a time like this."

"That's kind of you," I said.

"Is Mister Millett seeing visitors yet?"

"Not yet. We're hoping he'll be awake and ready for that soon. How's your family? Is Savannah doing better now that she's home?"

He glanced around at the strangers sitting in the waiting room.

He wanted privacy.

"Let's step outside," he said.

Buford Smike was just inside the hospital lobby intimidating everyone coming and going with the promise of violence in his eyes. Eustace, looking sinister, was standing outside by a late model four-door Chrysler. Bull Smike's sons were clearly packing and spoiling for the opportunity to draw and shoot.

"If only Otis and I had been as cautious as you," I said as we walked out to his car.

"I reckon we wasn't always so watchful, but there've been two attempts on my life over the years. We've learned to keep our guard up."

"Did you catch the men who tried to kill you?"

"They died trying. In one case we had some warning, and in the other we just outgunned 'em."

"Did you know who was behind the attempts?"

"We knew, but we couldn't prove it."

Eustace opened the back door for Bull Smike and me.

Buford waited by his open door, watching all

directions until Eustace got around to get behind the wheel. I would've sneered at all the cloak and dagger if Otis hadn't been up on the third floor in the emergency room.

When we were all in, I took off my sunglasses.

Buford looked over from the front and said, "Did Tooley do that to your face?"

"No," I said, "another one of Horner's thugs."

"I want his name," he said.

Buford knew how to treat a lady.

"I already took care of it," I said.

He cracked that smile that made his bad boy looks so appealing, and turned back to his job.

As the car pulled away, Bull Smike asked me for the details surrounding our brushes with Spider Jack Tooley.

When I was finished, he said, "He's wanted by the police in Oklahoma."

"For Lester's murder?"

"Yes, ma'am, and what the two of 'em did to the cops that night."

"The night they got away?"

"Yep. They set fire to their car. That's how they did it." I didn't understand, so he explained. "The police say it was bait. Someone sees the fire, stops to help, and gets their car hijacked. It so happened the police was the first to show up."

"They snatched a police vehicle?"

"They did for a fact. They knocked the coppers around, left 'em out there on the road, and drove off with their car. They dumped it, of course, stole something less noticeable, and were back in Texas before daylight."

I asked about Savannah again and was surprised to

learn that she had gotten her job back at Leo's Purple Turnip, a club over in south Dallas.

I said, "After all that's happened, you've let her come back here?"

Bull Smike bobbed his head in silence for a full minute before he said, "Even though I'm feeling more like Bronagh these days, I still can't be her jailer." He pushed back in his seat, and added, "She has to have her freedom if her life is to mean anything. She knows Travis Horner is not a nice man. She's gonna keep her distance."

"I don't mean to be rude," I said, "but that's dangerously naïve, Mister Smike. Otis is in the hospital hooked up to machines, and some of Travis Horner's men tried to kill me last night. He's a ruthless animal."

Bull Smike's one eye narrowed. "Of course he is, Miss. That's why my son Eustace has moved here to stay with his sister. It's the compromise I reached with my daughter. Eustace has my permission to shoot Travis Horner between the eyes if he as much as speaks to Savannah."

By the time Bull Smike and his sons dropped me off at the hospital, I had been given an envelope containing a substantial amount of cash as payment for our efforts in locating and attempting to bring Spider Jack Tooley to justice. I didn't want to accept the money, but Bull Smike insisted, saying he and Otis had reached an agreement and that he was a paying client.

However, when he tried to add keeping an eye on Savannah as part of our agreement, I found drawing a line easy by pulling from memory my short flight and crash landing courtesy of Gorgeous George Bittmer.

I told him, "We're investigators, Mister Smike, not bodyguards. But as a favor to you and your family, I'll drop by now and again where Savannah works…see what's up. If she needs my help, she has it."

27

OTIS WOKE UP that evening and started talking to proud doctors and pleased nurses. He wasn't anywhere near his old self, but I was willing to accept a weak and slightly confused partner with the promise that he would grow stronger and more lucid with time and attention.

"They ain't gonna tell me nothin', are they?" he said when he knew we were alone.

"Doc McGraw will find out," I said. "He'll tell us."

"Don't remember seein' him."

"He and Loretta were by before you were awake."

"You got a shiner, huh?"

"Yeah."

"You didn't get shot."

"Just you, big guy."

"I don't want you gettin' hurt." He stretched his mouth about. "My tongue feels like a side of beef. Can't seem to talk right."

"Mmmm."

"They got me on drugs." He looked away for a long moment. "They probably won't let me have a smoke."

"Probably not," I said.

"Probably not," he said, and brought his gaze back to me. "I was in a hospital once in London."

"You've been to London?"

"Yep. The Army sent me there."

"You never told me that."

"I got hit near a place called Bastogne...it was colder'n a banker's heart...just after Christmas '44." He squinted and stared at me. "What happened to your eye?"

"Nothing important. I think I'll put some makeup over it to trim the curiosity."

"Get some sirloin good and cold and lay it on there. You don't want your face lookin' like a baboon's hiney."

"No, I guess I wouldn't want that," I said, and we laughed.

That was mostly how it went. Chitchat. It was a while before Otis asked about who shot him.

"The boys downtown are matching some bullets. That might tell us who."

"Nobody got caught."

I shook my head. "Nope. Jack Tooley's still on the loose, if that's what you want to know."

"There was a baby girl," he said.

"They named her after you. They call her Millie."

It was just humming machinery for a stretch of time while he gazed at me. I was afraid he didn't understand until tears came to his eyes.

He said, "She's gonna get a good education, Missy. That's how gals go places and get what's theirs. Education."

I broke more than hospital rules when I got out of my chair and gave my partner a kiss on his cheek.

"We're turnin' to mush," he said. "We're doomed."

After Otis fell asleep, I sat there with an icepack on my face and kept him and his beeping machinery company as the starched white uniforms floated about.

I thought about how much I loved him and Henry, which was as much as I wanted on my mind at that time.

Speak of the devil.

Henry showed up looking tired and concerned. We left the hospital to find a place to eat.

"What kind of name is Cooty?" he wanted to know as we crossed the street.

"A nickname. Did he work out?"

"Last one go home. You bet he work out good."

There was a café down a half block or so and I watched everywhere as we walked there. Henry noticed me looking around and kept his eyes open, too.

Once we were in a corner booth inside the café and had ordered burgers and fries, he said, "Madame Li told me about last night. I think so. Kill you and Otis first. Get woman when you out of way. Find thing last."

"Savannah never had anything with her, Henry, only the clothes on her back."

"Maybe she *never* have thing. Just know where thing is."

"That makes sense. But there's something strange about all this."

"Always something strange."

"Travis Horner has given her some pricey gifts. He's a womanizer, so I guess he provides his dates nice restaurants and shows and maybe even gifts, but I'm sure he's not selecting delicate items in platinum for every woman he sleeps with."

"You think he love piano player?"

"Yeah. Love and jealousy is what it feels like to me…and it puts a weird twist to everything."

"Maybe not love, Baby Girl. If Travis Horner love bootlegger daughter, he come get her, he not trust killers to bring back."

"You've got a point there…except he might if he were angry enough."

"Then something bad happen," Henry said. "Lover spit."

"Spat," I said.

"Lover spat?"

"Yeah. Maybe they quarreled over the thing," I said.

"Did redhead tell something?"

"When we went to the hotel in Oklahoma City, she was afraid that we might leave her with Horner. Otis had to reassure her. I hadn't been with her much and wasn't reading her very well, so there might have been signs I missed. But she didn't say anything straight out about an argument."

"She drink you say."

"Downs vodka like water, and acts like a sex kitten with every man she meets, then becomes a thirteen-year-old for her daddy. Something else, she reacts to violence like she's at a stage play. With a mother like hers, maybe she's used to it. She cried about Lester's death, though, then got over it fast. And, come to think of it, she shed some tears when Otis beat up Horner, or, she drank her vodka too fast. I don't know, Henry. The thing is, there are enough inconsistencies to make me wonder who she really is."

"Lies of omission," he said.

"Where'd you get that?"

"Sergeant Friday say on *Dragnet*."

"Well, you're probably right. I think there are things she's not talking about. She acted more adult with her cousin Lester than anyone else I saw her talk to."

"Maybe Travis Horner kill her, too, after he find where thing is."

That put a shiver up my spine.

"You finish fries?"

I pushed my plate toward him. "You're welcome to them. I don't seem to have an appetite lately."

The next morning I was at Ivy's Beauty Shop when she opened. I brought coffee and sweet rolls to help soften the shock of my decision to come clean with her.

Ivy had a slim build, a sweet face, and the prim appearance of a Sunday school teacher. However, she belted out a laugh so raw and bawdy she could embarrass truck drivers. For the past several years she had regularly cut my hair and once even colored it. She had fitted me for wigs, advised me on all aspects of beauty and fashion, and occasionally held me down long enough to manicure my nails and apply some makeup.

I trusted her because she was as candid as a big sister and had never given me bad advice.

"God all hemlock," she said. "What happened to your face?"

"I was hit by a man who was trying to kill me."

Her laugh rattled the plate glass window.

"Now, what really happened?"

"We need to talk," I said.

Less than an hour later, Ivy knew what I did for a living and many of the stories behind the scars and bruises she had always thought I'd received working on a ranch.

"When you didn't dish the dirt with the rest of the girls, I figured you just lived a dull life and had nothing to yak about. How wrong I was, dear. How wrong I was."

During my confession, she washed and cut my hair and applied enough makeup to the bruise on my face that her first customer didn't even notice it when she arrived.

"I'm gonna give you what you need to keep covered up," she said when I was ready to leave, "but you'll make a mess of it. So, get into to see me every other day or so. If you can't do that, scrub your face clean and live with it or you'll look like you wandered away from a funny farm. All right, Nancy?"

"Nancy?" I asked, as I headed for the door.

"From now on you're Nancy Drew to me."

She must have deafened her next customer; I could hear her laughter halfway down the block.

28

I SPENT A good part of the day at the office.

Madame Li had installed new doors and locks every-where. Her cleaning crew and painters had been in as well, so other than our new leather sofa being gone, the place actually looked better than it had before what she referred to as the *incident* had occurred.

I hated to admit it, but I missed the smell of my part-ner's coffee and cigarettes.

I got Sidecar Sanchez on the phone and let him know what happened to Otis. I also asked if he would please keep his ear to the ground in reference to the whereabouts of Spider Jack Tooley, surreptitiously, of course.

"I am always a man of stealth," he replied, revealing his appreciation for my having used a five-dollar word.

Lee came by in a strange mood. It seemed clear to me that he wanted to discuss something, but wasn't sure how to get it going.

I had a lot on my mind, so while he was working out

his plan of attack, I asked if he knew a club in South Dallas called Leo's Purple Turnip.

"I think they call themselves a lounge," he said.

"What do you call them?"

"It's a pickup joint, dark, lots of mirrors, easy music. What's your interest in that place?"

"A client mentioned that the music was nice," I said, avoiding the truth. "I'm thinking of checking it out."

We talked some more. Damned if I can remember what about. Lee never got to it, but I knew it was about us. We were kind of back together, but it was the sex, it wasn't because we'd worked out what was keeping us from taking that last step.

And now, of course, there was the business of me needing to talk to someone about my habit of casually killing folks.

"I have no illusions," I said when Henry came by and I still had Lee's visit on my mind. "Lee's a cop and he takes it seriously."

"Millett Agency take work seriously," Henry said.

"Sure we do, but we work on the edge of the law, and you know it. It gets blurry out there where Otis and I deal with things. Sometimes, like Otis getting shot and me being ambushed, there're things we can discuss with the police. But cops have a hard time with our line of work."

"Client work secret. You never tell Lee?"

"It's not as if I go out to break laws, but laws get broken. Lee can't be the kind of cop he wants to be, know I'm breaking the law, and not do something about it."

"You never tell Lee what you do?"

"No, Henry, I don't. You and Otis know everything about me, what I do, what I've done, but no one else does."

"Family," Henry said.

"That's it," I said.

"So Lee not family."

"I think I want him to be, but how can I ask that of him?"

"Trust is issue, Baby Girl. Otis and Henry know everything and die without telling. We family."

"Exactly."

"Baby Girl decide for Lee? Or Lee decide for Lee?"

"If I open the door, it can never be closed, can it? There are others involved...you, Otis. I have to make the decision for Lee."

Henry watched me for a long moment before he said, "Lee you friend, good friend, but not family. Don't worry. Accept friendship or say goodbye."

Leo's Purple Turnip was in a brick building decorated with neon in an older section of South Dallas that was noted for jazz clubs and fried chicken, ribs, and catfish joints. The area was enjoying a renaissance. Some new eateries called pizza pie parlors were springing up and bringing a younger crowd. With its music and neon lights and foot traffic, I'd heard the district called Bourbon Street West.

I drove one of our rust buckets, a '51 Buick Roadmaster that had a great engine and good tires, but had the oxidized paint and dented fenders of a junker on its last trip to the store. Driving the old thing helped keep me invisible, but made me miss my new Olds 88 that was gathering dust in the parking lot at the hotel in Oklahoma City.

I arrived an hour before the Turnip's closing time and snagged a spot at the curb across and down the street. I had a clean view of the front door and the parking lot entrance. With the people and cars coming and going, no one noticed me sitting there with an ice pack on my eye. The blinking lights reflecting off my windows created a kind of camouflage, as well.

Lee was working a homicide on the other side of the city and left a message at the hospital to let me know he wasn't going to join me. He knew I spent a few hours with Otis every evening.

That night the talk in Emergency had been about transferring my partner to a regular room. The doctors didn't want to rush, but Otis was becoming less dependent on machinery that was needed by others.

"Don't get excited," one of the doctors told me, "We're days away from that move."

Savannah and Eustace came out of the Turnip shortly after closing, walked around to the parking lot, and drove out in a half-ton pickup.

I was careful about tailing them. I wanted to make sure no one else was following us. I wanted to stay alive in what had become a deadly game.

Savannah and her brother had supper at a truck stop that had a reputation for good steaks and chops. I stayed in my car, watched them through the diner windows, and had a Dr Pepper that I'd kept cold in the bucket of ice I'd brought for my ice pack.

Afterward, they drove over to Fort Worth to a garage apartment behind an eight-unit apartment building on a corner property in a clean, nicely tended working class neighborhood. Eustace parked at the curb.

The only obvious concern I saw exhibited for Savannah's safety was the sawed-off shotgun her brother carried by his leg.

I could see from where I'd stopped down the street that she hid her door key under a potted plant on the porch near the top of the stairs.

"Amateurs," Otis would've said.

I watched lights come on as they moved from room to room, gave them a few minutes, and then rolled by with my windows down. I heard her at the piano and thought the apartment was well suited for someone with her hours and the habit of playing music at 2:30 a.m.

A drive around the neighborhood and through the alley by her building familiarized me with the area before I drove away.

Having the Fort Worth and Dallas Police Departments actively searching for Spider Jack Tooley made me feel a little easier about moving around town. I was keeping my guard up, of course, but maybe the killing of the three men at the office plus the heat on Tooley was slowing Travis Horner down a bit.

When I mentioned my theory to Henry, he said, "Travis Horner not slow down because men die."

"No?" I said.

"He slow down when he get thing he want. He make new plan now and come again. You watch all direction all time. Travis Horner sick dog."

I took Henry at his word and became extra careful as I went to and from the office and home and hospital and Ivy's for makeup lessons. I was especially watchful at nights when I staked out the Turnip.

At first, I did pretty much what I did that first time when I followed Savannah and her brother home. I wanted to make sure no one else was following them.

When I felt more confident about how my face looked, I began entering the lounge an hour or so before closing wearing my Bettie Page wig and clear glass horn-rimmed glasses with my short black jacket, black cotton turtleneck, black slacks, and black boots.

It was a dark place with high-backed private booths, soft music, softer conversation, and the not unpleasant aroma of the popular grilled shrimp appetizer plates they served. I found I could sit at the far side of the bar across the room from where Savannah played piano and, with the help of the many mirrors, see the entrance and people coming and going everywhere in the room.

Also, because I sat back there, I was rarely propositioned by trolling strangers. Or maybe the lack of male attention was because I looked like a black widow. That was a possibility, too.

The bartender called me his lady in black, quickly learned that I nursed Dr Pepper in a highball glass, and never allowed me to pay for a drink.

Eustace sat a few stools from me and looked over from time to time. He didn't know who I was, and I saw no reason to tell him.

That evening, when it was nearing closing time and I was preparing to leave, I noticed Eustace react to something.

He was normally a statue.

I used the mirror behind the bar to find out what caught his interest, and my heart rate picked up.

Travis Horner stood near the entrance talking with

a couple of guys. One was Dapper Dan, the man who opened the door to Travis' room at the Skirvin Hotel. I didn't know the other one, a tough-looking customer.

Travis wrote something on a matchbook cover and gave it to the man I didn't know, then turned into the room and limped after the hostess to a booth. Good. He was still suffering from the damage Otis did to his ankle that night in the hotel room.

Dapper Dan followed his slimy boss to a booth; the other man left.

I made a decision.

Eustace was there to protect his sister.

I got up and followed the tough-looking guy who'd been given the matchbook cover. He seemed the most likely candidate for some dirty work.

The man with the matchbook cover drove a late model Pontiac and was easy to keep in sight from several cars back. He was on his way to Fort Worth and made all the expected turns until my suspicion that he was going to Savannah's apartment became my belief.

When I had the opportunity to pass him without calling attention to myself, I did so. Then I put the steam on to get to her apartment ahead of him.

Unless I'd made a mistake and he was going somewhere else, I figured I would get to her place at least ten minutes ahead of him. I wondered if the plan was for this guy to get the drop on Eustace when he and his sister arrived home.

I put my clunker down the street a couple of houses, left my horn-rimmed glasses and my purse in the car, ran back and up the stairs, and found the key under the pot of pink geraniums. After opening the front door, I put the key back.

Inside the apartment, I cleaned away my prints with my handkerchief, closed and locked the door behind me, and paused an instant to get my bearings. I could see by the dim light from the small lamp near the sofa that the layout of the wall-to-wall carpeted apartment was straightforward.

I moved at once past a table and chairs in the dining room into the kitchen where I unlocked and opened the back door. I checked to make sure there was nothing to block a fast exit down the back stairs, then wedged a piece of folded paper towel into the door latch. The door, in a closed position, would open if it were pulled, no turning of the knob necessary.

I cleaned my prints from the door and kept the handkerchief in my hand as I opened the fridge, which held little more than beer. Unwashed dishes were piled in and around the sink. A skillet and pot that needed cleaning were on the stove.

Bachelors.

Coming back through the long living room, I was careful to stay back from the windows as I crossed to the doorway that led to a short hall and two bedrooms separated by a bathroom.

I could see by window light that Savannah's brother's room was neat. The bed was made. His closet was full with some of his clothes and Savannah's overflow.

Savannah's bedroom was the larger of the two. Her low dresser was a mess on top and had several drawers open. Her closet was full. Clothes were piled on an upholstered chair, hanging from the edges of a freestanding, full-length mirror, and sticking out from beneath her unmade bed.

I'd arrived early, toured the apartment, and fixed myself an emergency exit. All that remained to do was to find out what assignment Travis' man had been given. In fact, I wanted the guy to answer a couple of questions for me.

I moved to the hallway to wait. There was no decent place for an ambush in the apartment, but the hallway was darker than the other rooms and had a good view of the front door. The only drawback was there was no exit on that side of the apartment.

As it got later, I worried that I'd guessed wrong, until I heard someone at the front door. My heart lurched. I hadn't heard a car door close or someone coming up the stairs, but there he was.

I got a .38 in my hand, cocked it, and stepped back into the darkness.

29

THE MATCHBOOK MAN entered, bringing the faint, tangy odor of barbeque with him. He'd stopped for something to eat on his way.

He closed the door without making a sound.

His was a deliberate action when he placed the key on the end table by the door, and when he turned his head to scan the room. He was looking, listening, smelling. I didn't think he'd been in Savannah's apartment before and he was a cautious man.

I remained still and watched his every move by the dim light from the little lamp. I didn't think he could see me, since I was back from the doorway, totally in darkness, and his eyes were still adjusting to the new situation. But I guessed even if he saw me, he wouldn't react. Travis had grown tired of fools. He'd paid for a real pro. My nerves were tingling.

He was taller than I was, but not by much, and casually dressed with taste—loafers, sport shirt, lightweight jacket, all in shades of brown. He looked mid-thirties, with dark, close-cut hair, a thick neck, and broad shoulders. He had muscle under that haberdashery, and weapons, too, but a true tailor had rendered all that invisible. Success and confidence.

His cold eyes and hard face held a threat. *Il cherche la bagarre,* my dad would've said of that face. And I would say he'd come to the right place to look for a fight.

"Always shoot first," Albert Sun Man Ramirez had advised me.

I brought up my pistol. I was ready to step out of the darkness and confront the matchbook man when I heard car doors slamming and Savannah's voice. There was another voice, too.

A man spoke to someone and then maybe to Savannah as they walked across the wide driveway toward the stairs. That was my interpretation, at least. I was across the room from the closest window.

Matchbook man walked over to the window, looked down, and then moved to the center of the living room and took a stance to wait. He was a poser who thought he was alone. If he had a weakness, it was vanity.

The conversation continued as Savannah and others came up the stairs. Out of the jumble of sounds, the only thing I heard clearly was when she said, "The key's not here," in that pretty Ozark drawl.

The door opened and Savannah, Travis Horner, and young Dapper Dan entered.

"Just like magic," she said, and turned in a circle.

I had a bad feeling about Eustace. Where was he? What had happened to him?

I felt my pulse quicken, my anger welling up. Here was the man who had sicced his killers on Otis and me, and I had the drop on him. I could kill him and two of his cronies before any of them could draw a weapon.

I tensed up, preparing for action.

But Savannah was everywhere. She was certain to get hurt if I opened fire.

She was glimmering about the men, a redheaded butterfly in a sheath of gold sequins, talking, touching, waving her hands, carrying on like a—she was drunk. That was it.

Travis put her little gold pocketbook on the end table near the door key, and took her by the arm. He said, "We were talking about your suitcase, Savannah."

She jerked away from him. "I want out of this dress." She took an awkward step or two, threatening to lose her balance.

Dapper Dan caught her before she fell, and she laughed.

"Turn on that lamp and then wait in the car," Travis told Dapper Dan, who released his hold on Savannah.

"I wanna change my dress." She said, and vamped a step or two, flirting with the matchbook man.

I eased back into the shadow as light was added to the living room.

Dapper Dan left and I was down to eliminating two bad guys if Savannah ever stopped staggering about, and if the three ever strayed far enough apart to give me clean targets.

I'd shut down the hired man first and worry about Travis second. He didn't appear to be carrying. I would assume he was, of course, and shoot him dead in his tracks. I had a good feeling about my plan.

Dapper Dan would be a world away. If he were stupid enough to come back upstairs, he'd be alone with the bodies, because Savannah and I would be out the back door and gone.

"Why don't we talk about the suitcase while you're

changing," Travis suggested to Savannah in a tone of voice reserved for drunks and obstreperous children.

"Who're you?" she asked the matchbook man.

She reached for him, but he sidestepped her and she moved between him and me and did a little dance step.

"His name's Dale," Travis said, and took her by the arm once again. He turned her toward where I was standing in the hall.

It wasn't working. They weren't allowing me the opportunity.

I had to get out of sight fast or be prepared to play rough with Savannah in the mix. I was on the wrong side of the apartment to excuse myself and leave by the back door. The bathroom was too small for hiding and waiting, plus I had a feeling the intoxicated pianist was going to be in there sooner or later throwing up.

I retreated into her bedroom, knowing that if she were going to change clothes, she'd be in there soon, too. It was either that or take out Travis as he came into the hall and do my best to get Savannah out of the danger zone when the matchbook man began throwing lead. Nailing Travis first was the wrong way to do it and hope to stay safe.

Out of sight didn't mean safe.

There wasn't a wall in that apartment that would stop a bullet from the weapons the matchbook man was no doubt carrying. I knew they wouldn't stop my slugs.

I'd boxed myself in.

I'd already seen that the closet in Savannah's bedroom was stuffed full. I scanned the room, came to a conclusion, and hustled around to the far side of the bed, the side that was near the wall. I dropped to the floor and eyeballed the narrow space beneath the low-slung bedsprings. I wasn't certain I could get under there.

I was stretching out on my back as I heard Savannah in the hallway, laughing. My heart was slamming against my ribs. Attacking would've made the most sense, since I would've had the upper hand, but I couldn't risk Savannah's life—hell, my own life— unless I could do it right.

Shit!

I couldn't remember ever feeling more vulnerable as I scooted under the bed. It was crowded with boxes and shoes and piles of clothing. But most of that had been pushed in from the other side. There was room for me, but just barely.

I held my pistol in my hand by my side. I had so little freedom of movement I would've blown a toe off if I'd tried to use it. My nose had a slight clearance. I could just turn my head to the side to watch their feet as Savannah and Travis entered.

"Enough playing around," Travis growled. "Now I want the suitcase."

I saw her feet as she kicked off her heels.

"It's not here," she growled back and giggled. "If you don't believe me, look around."

Where Travis stood, I could see that one of his shoes was cut open to accommodate his bandaged foot and ankle. He favored that foot when he moved.

"I couldn't find an elephant in this mess." She giggled some more and he added, "My box better be in your suitcase."

"It is. Unzip, please."

"You should have had two suitcases. God knows you left plenty of clothes behind."

"I could've taken more except for that ol' box."

"What that box has in it is important to me, Savannah."

"Lester said that."

"I'll bet he did."

Her dress fell in a circle around her ankles and she stepped out of it. I pictured her in panties and bra as I had seen her the night I met her at Curly's Tavern.

He went on, "So where is it, damn it? Will you just tell me that?"

"Why're you mad at me? I didn't want your old box."

"Why'd you take it then?"

She left her dress where it fell. I watched her bare feet go to her dresser and heard her open a drawer.

"I didn't take it."

"Savannah, make sense. You said it was in your suitcase. The suitcase I bought you. Right or wrong?"

"I love that suitcase, Travis."

Savannah took something from the drawer. A negligee, maybe. I could see the bottom of the sheer garment flare out as she slipped it on and turned in front of the full-length mirror.

"I'm glad you do, sweetie, but now I want to know where it is."

"It's where Lester told me to put it."

"Oh? Now we're getting somewhere."

"You said we were going to Paris."

"We will, honey. We will. But now, let's think about where Lester told you to put your suitcase. Okay?"

"Amarillo is not Paris, Travis. Even Dallas is not Paris."

"Where did Lester put your suitcase, sweetie? Do you remember?"

"I put it. He didn't put it."

"Where did *you* put it then?"

"You aren't really going to take me to Paris, are you?"

"Savannah, we're very close here. Can we just concentrate on one thing at a time?"

"I'm concentrating on Paris."

I was startled when Savannah collapsed onto the bed above me. Travis stepped over and stood beside her. I saw her hand dangling over the edge of the bed, her manicured nails almost touching the carpeted floor.

"You can't go to sleep now. We're talking."

"You're talking. I'm kind of listening."

"Tell me where Lester told you to put the suitcase and I'll go away and you can get some sleep. Okay?"

"At the bus station."

Just like that.

"The bus station?"

"Uh huh."

"You checked your suitcase at the bus depot?"

"Lester told me to do that first thing, so no one would talk me out of it. First thing, he said."

"Do you have the claim check?"

"What's that?"

"The ticket they gave you when you checked your suitcase."

"It has a number on it?"

"That's it. Do you have it?"

"It's in my pocketbook."

"Wonderful. Can you get it for me?"

"I don't know where it is."

"I don't understand."

"I must've lost it."

"You lost your purse?"

"I guess so. I don't know where it is."

"In this mess it could be anywhere. Okay, think hard, Savannah. Which purse did you have with you?"

"My red clutch. It goes with my red dress."

My heart leaped.

I had her red clutch bag. It was in the pocket of my leather jacket, the jacket that had a bullet hole in the sleeve. It was in the trunk of my car in the lot at the Skirvin Hotel in Oklahoma City.

Travis said, "Get it for me, will you? Get up and get it."

"I don't know what happened to it. I had it with me when I was with Lester, and then that man shot Lester."

"Damn that Spider. I asked him to do one simple thing for me."

"I had it before he started dragging me around and then I didn't have it."

"God damn that Spider. You had it, didn't you, honey? You had it and Spider messed it up. You see, I have to do everything myself."

Travis limped around in a tight circle.

"All right. I'll get it," he said. "I'll go there and buy my way past that claim check shit. Now we're talking about the suitcase I bought you, right? Light brown leather with straps?"

"Travis?"

"Yes, honey?"

"I told Lester he shouldn't take your box, but he said

you'd pay him to get it back. That's why he took it."

"I know. I know, Savannah. It wasn't your fault. It's just gone too far now, that's all." He exhaled with relief. "The damn bus depot. Okay. Give me a kiss."

He leaned over the bed and I guessed they kissed.

"You close your eyes now. You look so pretty with your head on the pillow. I want to always remember you that way. Goodnight, Savannah."

Always remember you?

"Another kiss, Travis."

He leaned over the bed for another kiss, a longer one.

"Can't you stay?"

"Not tonight, dear. Not tonight."

"I wish you could."

"Goodnight, Savannah."

"Goodnight, Travis."

Travis limped away and I heard the front door close.

A moment or so later, if I hadn't been watching Savannah's hand that was again hanging down beside the bed, I would not have seen the brown loafers. I would not have known that Dale, the matchbook man, had entered the bedroom. The man was a cat burglar.

And then a chill hit me.

I understood why he was there and my heart lurched so hard I had to suppress an impulse to gasp. I could do nothing to help her.

The matchbook man would kill me before I could struggle out from beneath the bed, and I was too confined to move my pistol to the angle I needed to shoot him. I should've taken care of him when I had the chance.

"Savannah," Dale said.

"Yes?" she said.

"I want you to open your eyes," he said. "I want you to look at me."

I saw her hand slide under the bed and it happened fast.

There were three shots fired.

I almost came out of my skin from the noise of the three blasts that were discharged so close together.

It took a moment to register that a bullet had come through the mattress and smacked hard into the floor above my shoulder, right next to my neck.

The springs above my face responded as Savannah jumped up and ran from the bedroom. I saw motion where Dale, the matchbook man, had been standing.

I struggled out, got to my feet, and took two strides straight across the bed. Out of the corner of my eye, I saw Dale dead on the floor, a poser to the end with his head resting in a nimbus of golden sequins.

Savannah had stashed a pistol beneath the bed and had gotten off two shots to his one. Of course. She was a Smike from the Ozarks. She was probably born with a gun in her hand.

I ran into the living room. The front door stood open.

Through the ringing in my ears, I heard gunshots from the street below. I hurried out to the front porch.

Dapper Dan was behind the wheel of the car pulling away, the car at which Savannah was shooting as she ran barefoot across the wide driveway, her baby blue negligee billowing out behind her.

I don't know if she hit Travis Horner, but she emptied her revolver giving it a try.

When I got to her, she was on her knees, crying. I took

her weapon, jammed it in my belt, helped her to her feet, and guided her down the street.

Behind us, windows in the front apartments were lighting up, and by the time we'd reached my car, a porch light had come on at one of the houses across the street.

It was 3:00 a.m.

With luck, we would be halfway to Broken Bow before the police had a handle on what happened at Savannah's garage apartment.

30

SAVANNAH SLEPT UNTIL I woke her for directions, and then stayed awake for the rest of the drive over the back roads north and east of Broken Bow.

I don't know that I have ever been in a more beautiful place than the wooded hills of southeast Oklahoma at daybreak. When I pulled to the side of the road to remove my Bettie Page wig and change into a Levi's jacket, I stood for a long while in the gentle light streaming through the trees. There was tranquility in those clean scented woods, something I needed more of, something that would have to wait.

"Soft wood grows on one side of the hills and hard wood grows on the other," Savannah instructed me the moment I returned to the car.

She was happy to be near home and delighted to tell me about trees and identify the many rushing creeks we crossed and point out and name the distant hills emerging from the morning haze.

She seemed to have forgotten the events of the past night. At least she didn't mention them.

A chorus of coonhounds ran around the car greeting us as I drove up.

Bronagh walked out to meet us wearing a simple housedress. She was barefoot and her hair was pulled back in a ponytail that made her look younger than her fifty years.

She'd been waiting for us with a blanket in her arms. I'd telephoned her from Broken Bow to let her know her daughter was on her way home, and that she was wearing a negligee.

"Wrap up in this, Savannah. There are hands about."

"Yes, Mama," Savannah said and draped the light cotton blanket over her shoulders for the walk across the yard, past the crowded birdbath, up the steps, across the porch, and into the house. The dogs stopped at the bottom of the steps.

Bronagh said to me, "The kitchen's straight back. Help yourself to coffee." To Savannah, she said, "I've drawn you a hot tub and laid out some fresh clothes."

There was more, but we were walking in different directions and her voice faded. I felt it deep inside, the memory of my own mother, the selfless giving. She was everything to me until she was too sick to even care for herself.

I was young; Aunt Dora, Mom's sister, came to stay with us until my dad finally returned home.

All that came rushing back because of the kitchen smells, the tidy house, the pictures of family here and there. What did I think the home of a bootlegger would be like? Not what I'd just discovered.

Bronagh entered the kitchen and said, "You found the coffee."

"I did. Thank you."

"You must be exhausted," she said and poured a cup for herself and added to mine.

"It's been a long night," I said. "But this will bring me around."

"Do you mind sitting at the kitchen table or would you rather…"

"I prefer being here, thanks."

We sat down across from each other, our coffee cups and a plate of scones and butter between us.

"I'll get us started," Bronagh said. "What happened?"

Why didn't I just say that Travis Horner has hired killers to murder us all? He will continue trying to kill us until he succeeds or we kill him.

Maybe it was the aroma of freshly baked scones.

I didn't know, but instead of being plainspoken, I said, "Savannah has survived an attempt on her life, Mrs. Smike."

"Bronagh, please. Your name's Kristin, isn't it?"

I nodded.

"Why would anyone want to kill my daughter?" Bronagh said, containing her anger.

"I don't know exactly why."

"You know who?"

Her voice was taking on an edge.

"Savannah shot and killed the man who tried to murder her," I said, still sidestepping straight talk.

"Good," Bronagh said.

"He was a hired gun," I parceled out.

"And you know who hired him, don't you?"

"I do. Let me say this first. Savannah acted in self-defense. She'd surely be found innocent in the eyes of the law if she were to go before a judge."

"She'll never see a judge," Bronagh said. "Any witnesses?"

"None," I said, since I alone knew the truth, and I saw no need to share it.

"Will the police find a weapon with my daughter's fingerprints?"

"No," I said.

I'd thrown her pistol in the Red River that morning, another fact that didn't need sharing.

"You're sure?"

"Positive."

Bronagh nodded.

"And another thing," I said.

"Yes?"

"The man she shot was a thug. There's a limit to how much effort Fort Worth will expend on his behalf."

"That's true, isn't it? But tell me, Kristin, I'm grateful, please don't misunderstand, but why did you bring her home instead of calling the police?"

"You're my client, not the police. If you want to speak to them, that's your affair."

Bronagh smiled and took a deep breath. "Now I understand why Buford likes you. You're smart as well as pretty."

I felt my cheeks grow warm.

"You haven't mentioned Eustace," Bronagh said. "Where was he? Do you know?"

"I saw him last at the club where Savannah works. I don't know after that."

Bronagh sighed. "It has become more difficult every year just to sell whiskey, and then Luther let Savannah talk him into her leaving home. It was bad enough rounding her up from her run-aways, but our lives have become a nightmare since he told her she could come and go at will. Sometimes it seems Buford's the only one around here with a lick of common sense."

Our talk had become gossip. I pushed my chair back.

"I hope you won't think I'm being rude, Bronagh…"

"But you need to go."

"I'm afraid so."

"But not before telling me who hired the man who tried to kill our Savannah. Luther will want to know."

I was another three hours plus getting to Oklahoma City. I stopped for coffee twice and stayed awake by strength of will.

I felt certain Horner would drive up himself to handle the matter of retrieving his box of papers. And, of course, something that he wanted back so badly was something I wanted to keep him from getting, if I possibly could.

When did he leave Fort Worth? That was the question. I'd driven like a bat out of hell, but since I'd taken the long way by delivering Savannah, the chances were slim I'd get to the bus depot first.

I did have a couple of advantages, though. Horner didn't know he was in a race, and he thought the suitcase would be secure at the bus depot until he arrived to request it.

31

WHEN I REACHED the Skirvin Hotel parking lot, I produced the parking stub, paid the fee, and made a long-term deal for the rust bucket I was leaving behind.

"Let's hope she starts," the attendant said about my dust-covered Olds. "She's been a long spell just sittin' here."

I opened the trunk before I tested the battery. I took Savannah's little handbag from the pocket of my leather jacket, removed the luggage claim check, and was treated to a wonderful surprise.

The claim check was for the luggage room at the Greyhound Bus Depot in Amarillo, Texas.

It took me a moment, but I worked it out.

Lester knew Savannah would be an easy mark for some bus station hustler when she arrived in Oklahoma City. That's why he'd told her to check her bag first thing when she arrived at the bus depot, and that's what she did.

She checked her suitcase as soon as she walked into the bus station in Amarillo, before she boarded the

Greyhound that took her to Oklahoma City.

First thing, Lester had said.

I could picture that slimy Horner losing his temper when his redhead's suitcase wasn't where it was supposed to be. And there he was with all his bridges burned.

I was laughing when I hit the starter and my Olds 88 woke up like it had never been asleep. The parking lot attendant must've thought I'd gone loony, because I was still laughing when I left the hotel parking lot and entered downtown traffic.

Since I no longer had any need to go to the bus depot in Oklahoma City, I headed out of town. Route 66 wasn't hard to find, and I even managed to get a few miles west of the city before I finally couldn't stay awake any longer.

I pulled into the next motel I came to, a quaint gathering of freshly painted little houses called Sleepy Haven. Before entering the office to register, I snooped around the grounds, just a quick look in case I had to exit fast.

I didn't think I was being followed, but that didn't mean there wasn't a tail on me. I was determined to stay alert and double watch my hiney, as Otis would say.

The manager, a balding grandpa in thick glasses and a wrinkled shirt, smelled like cigarettes and had a hacking cough. The drone of TV voices and audience laughter came from the other room.

"We pass inspection?" he asked from behind a speckled Formica counter.

I didn't say anything.

"What was you lookin' for, a swimmin' pool?"

I remained silent.

After I signed in, he turned the guest register around and read aloud. "Nan Drew."

He stared at me while he coughed, his glasses enlarging his rheumy eyes. When he was able, he said, "You come up from Texas, Miss Drew?"

I smiled.

"Seen your license plate," he said, pleased that he had finally gotten a reaction from me. He picked up the money I'd put on the counter. "This pays you up solid till tomorrow noon."

"You know of any youngsters that might want to wash my car?"

"I can call my daughter's boy," he said.

I placed three dollars on the counter. "Will that cover it?"

"More'n enough," Grandpa said and began to hack.

He hacked for a while, then spit into a wastebasket he picked up from below the counter. When he was finished, he handed me my room key.

"Number nine," he said, and threw his thumb the direction I was supposed to go.

He fired up a cigarette as I walked out.

Six hours later, I drove away from Sleepy Haven in a shiny car and feeling like a new girl. Even though the bed had been lumpy and the shower weak, I could've slept on spikes, I'd been so worn out.

I was wearing what I always wore, black denim, but everything was clean and fresh from my underwear out. Also, I'd cleaned and oiled my pistols, and counted the cash in the bag that Otis had been given to ransom Savannah at Curly's Tavern, lo those many fun-filled days ago.

The bag contained ten thousand dollars, another reason for Travis Horner to be mad at Otis. Somehow, though, I didn't think money was the issue.

My next task was to find a decent café. After that, it would be a straight line to Amarillo.

After passing a couple of places specializing in chicken fried steak, I gave in and pulled into the next roadside café promoting that Sooner specialty. Otis would've stopped at the first one and ordered mashed potatoes, peas, corn, biscuits, and extra gravy to go with it.

I could hear him saying, "What's the point of bein' in Oklahoma if you ain't gonna eat like an Okie?"

I used the payphone back by the restrooms to give Henry a call. I hadn't spoken to him since I'd stopped for gas in Broken Bow.

"You hear Smike boy die in shootout?"

Damn it.

"No, I hadn't heard that. What're the details?"

"Outside Turnip club. Smike boy kill two men. They kill him."

I wasn't surprised, but it didn't make it any easier. He was Bronagh's youngest.

"Men start, Smike boy finish."

I felt my blood begin to boil. I didn't need another reason to despise Travis Horner, but I had one. I changed the subject.

"Are you seeing Otis every day?"

"Every day. Otis grumble to go home."

Grumble?

"I'm sure he does. What do his doctors say?"

"Soon."

"Uh huh. Well, I really will be home soon. I know how busy you are, Henry."

"Otis like brother."

"It's a long drive, though."

"Jim go, too. Make drive easier."

"How's that big dog?"

"Eat me out house and home. Maybe come stay with you."

Technically, Jim was mine. But Henry had spent more time with him and would never give him up. I'd heard Henry having long conversations with him. Who knew the extent of the dog's vocabulary or exactly what he understood of life around him? He was great company out in that prairie country.

He was a loyal watchdog, too. That was important, since Henry was sometimes gone all day. At a hundred and ten pounds, a German shepherd was not a dog a stranger wanted to wrestle with, especially a dog as willing as Jim to defend his territory and protect his loved ones.

It was pushing 10:00 p.m. by the time I left my car parked on the brick street out front and walked into the Greyhound Bus Depot in Amarillo. I found the baggage storage room, gave the man there Savannah's claim check, paid the fee, and was given her light brown leather suitcase. No questions asked.

With her suitcase in the trunk of my car, I drove over to the El Coyote Motel.

Harlan and I used to stay there when we came to Amarillo to hustle pool. The motel was clean and well run and just down the street from the pool hall.

As I walked up, I saw Dolores, the owner, through the office window. She was hard to miss with her apricot-colored hair. She was sitting behind the front counter reading the paper with her glasses perched on her nose, and her cat Greta snuggled up near her.

She looked up when I opened the door and the little bell ding-a-linged.

She took off her glasses and said, "Well, bless your heart. Look who's here, Greta. Is your Uncle Harlan with you?"

"No, I'm by myself this time."

"So you didn't fly in?"

I shook my head. "Drove in."

Greta moved over so I could give her a scratch.

"That's just as well," she said. "Manfred's not here anymore to come pick you up at the airfield."

"Why's that, Dolores?"

"He left me, dear. Thanks to his friend Sam Two Bears."

"What happened?"

"Sam was hidin' out here for a while. He was duckin' a subpoena, see, so when he finally thought it was safe enough to hightail it, he took off, and Manfred went with him."

"I'm not sure I understand," I said.

"He was up to no good, that Sam Two Bears. Talked my Manfred into some silly scheme. They took as much money with 'em as they could get their hands on, but I had some woman's intuition about things. They was always drinkin' late and talkin' low, you know, like they thought I couldn't hear. But I did hear, all right. I gathered up the motel papers and cash and anything else I thought they might snitch and do mischief with and put it all where they couldn't get to it."

"Good for you."

"There was a commotion here the night they left; the two of 'em had their snoots full. I can tell you, they was breathin' tornadoes. I told Manfred he should be ashamed of hisself, and I told that wild Indian Sam Two Bears that unless he wanted me ringin' up the police, he'd better git while the gittin' was good."

"I'm glad you stuck up for yourself, Dolores."

"Thank you, dear. I was just ate up with crazy at first. But after seein' how much more profitable the motel is with him gone, I don't want 'im back. Oh, it's different, a girl your age, but I can do just fine without a man clutterin' up the place. Has to be some advantage to bein' fifty."

She'd celebrated fifty ten years ago.

"Dolores, you're teasing me. You're not fifty."

"If I didn't do my hair every couple of weeks, you'd see." She put on her glasses and looked at the register. "Kristin would like that quiet room around on the side, wouldn't she, Greta?"

"If it's available," I said.

My accommodation, which was at the side of El Coyote Motel, was one of only a few rooms there that had some privacy. The other rooms all faced the swimming pool—kids during the day and drunks at night.

I brought in and put away my things. I didn't travel with much, but there were always changes of clothes in the trunk. And some hardware, of course.

I'd had the time to do some thinking on the drive over from Oklahoma City and had come up with a plan of sorts. It would depend on some help I was going to ask of Andy Olsen, the owner of Andy's Snooker Palace. I remembered him as always being happy to share in our winnings when Harlan and I hustled at his place.

Savannah's suitcase could have been any one of her messy dresser drawers. With no attempt to fold anything, she'd stuffed clothing on all sides of a pewter-colored metal box.

The old metal container was about the size of my grandpa's fish and tackle box, except it had a flat lid and an inset lock. I got the lock pick set from the trunk of my car, along with a heavy screwdriver as a backup. Otis was skillful at picking locks, while I knew my limitations.

Fifteen minutes or so later, I'd almost lost my patience when the lock gave. I opened the lid and glanced in at the stacked and bundled papers as I replaced the picks I'd used and zipped up the little leather case that Otis had given me for my birthday last year.

The collection of papers and pictures Travis Horner had in that box ran from the mundane to the salacious. There were birth certificates, property deeds, insurance policies, bank statements, and loan records, as well as a couple of gold watches, a man's gold ring with a cracked diamond setting, and best of all, a book listing the names of all the corrupted officials on his payroll from Amarillo to Oklahoma City.

Another kind of insurance was represented, too, a collection of photographs of predominantly older men and young women having sex. Noted on the backs of these pictures were the names of the men and their titles; state senators and mayors were among the photo subjects.

It was midnight by the time I put everything away and went to bed.

Before breakfast the next morning, I wrapped Travis Horner's box in cardboard and addressed it to Henry Chin. After breakfast, I paid a visit to the beauty parlor where Dolores got her hair done. I had my nails done and my hair shampooed and trimmed, and then I went shopping.

I needed to freshen my look.

It took some searching to find black Levi's. "This ain't Dallas," one store owner told me. But I found an emporium that had them and purchased three of everything I needed. Dolores gave me the names of some stores where I found the cotton shirts I liked. I even got my boots shined to within an inch of their lives.

If anyone were going to be critical of Baby Shark, it would have to be about my game, not my appearance.

The Levi's needed to be laundered before I could wear them. I paid the woman who cleaned my room to do that for me, and she had them back by early afternoon, along with my new shirts ironed and on hangers.

Fresh and new was important, but broke in was essential, both for reputation and comfort. I needed at least a few miles on my new clothes, so I wore fresh Levi's to the post office that afternoon to mail Travis Horner's box to Henry.

I got looks and comments from the flyboys in town from the Air Force base. I hadn't expected that, but was happy to see *fresh* worked on more than one level.

I had a feeling that it was going to be okay over at Andy's Snooker Palace. I had to laugh, though, since I was concentrating so hard on appearance. I still had a blade in each boot, a .32 on my ankle, and a .38 in my purse.

I knew who I might have to deal with.

32

ANDY OLSEN, THE owner of Andy's Snooker Palace, looked a bit like a young Wallace Beery and even had the actor's slow, gruff way of speaking. That was the end of the comparison, though. Andy was a businessman and ran a serious pool hall.

"Amarillo is on Route 66," he liked to say. "We're at the crossroads of the Texas Panhandle. We never know who might drop in."

He had regulation tables, kept his large hall clean, the equipment in top shape, and attracted good players on their way to and from the coast.

There was nothing stuffy or pretentious about his pool hall, but he did hold one table in darkness in the back of the room for better players. Like a perfectly tuned concert piano, polished and standing by for special performances, the table was covered and always ready for the big game.

But Andy's was also a favorite hangout for the young airmen that were stationed nearby, and the local girls knew it. So, Andy put up a wall. He separated the Snooker

Palace into two sides: a burger joint/coffee shop on one and his tables on the other.

The attached burger joint was Andy's genius. The girls showed up in droves. The music and laughter created a not unpleasant, off-to-the-side, low volume din, and the tables were close enough for the young men to have somewhere to blow off energy and show off between burgers and Cokes.

It didn't take Andy long to sense the change in the poolroom when I entered. I saw him look up in advance of the whistles. He put away the paperwork he was doing because he could see a platinum blonde carrying a cue case was on her way back to see him.

As I approached the counter, I saw that he recognized me.

The room had gone quiet. Amarillo didn't get many surprises. They savored those that came their way.

Neither of us spoke for a long moment, and then he said, "You're a big girl now, Baby."

"Does that mean I get a big girl welcome?" I asked and offered him my cheek.

"Indeed it does," he said, and gave me a kiss.

The hormonal level that had been in ascendancy as I crossed the room peaked out with the kiss. The predictable raucous reaction of the young men was instant.

"You already have fans," Andy said as we moved away from the counter and over to a table and chairs where he ordered coffee and a Dr Pepper.

"You have a good memory, Andy."

"For some people. Have you come to play?"

"I want to talk to you about that."

"Is Harlan with you?"

"No. I'm by myself."

We were silent while the young waitress gave me the once over and put our coffee and Dr Pepper on the table. I thanked her and offered her a smile. I'd always gotten along with women.

She smiled in return, but she wasn't fully committed.

"You've seen him lately?" he asked.

"Well, you know, I haven't, Andy. We've both been busy."

Andy drank his coffee with cream. He was a moment or so with that chore, and then he said, "So? What's up?"

"There's someone local here I'd like to play. Perhaps you could arrange it."

"Harlan's not here, so I can assume this is on the up and up."

"You can assume that. Just some friendly nine ball. There'll be some action, of course."

"Not for anyone to see," he said. "You know my rules."

I took an envelope from my purse and placed it on his side of the table.

"Five grand to back up my play."

Andy wasn't easily taken off guard, but half the price of a three-bedroom tract home in the suburbs caught his attention. He looked at the envelope for a moment and then up at me. "And who's the local?"

"Travis Horner," I said. "He should pop five yards a match. Don't you think?"

"How do you know that worthless sonofabitch?"

There were a lot of things I could've told Andy, but I didn't see how it would benefit anyone.

I said, "I don't know him. I only know he brags about his pool game. That's the part that interests me."

"You want more than his money, Baby."

Andy had some busybody in him.

"Okay, what I really want to do is punish him for being a pathetic human being."

He liked that reply. "Does he know you?"

"You can introduce us. You gave me my nickname, you know."

"Yeah, Harlan told me I did. What was that? Four years ago? You were such an innocent thing when you used to come in with your dad."

"I was a lot younger, Andy."

"I know. Then you lost him and took up with Harlan."

"Harlan's not all that bad," I said.

"That's what you say, but you were coming in here and eating all the young players alive. What better name than Baby Shark?"

I shrugged. I'd been proving things in those days.

"Let's say Travis Horner's in town, when do you want to do this?"

"Give me a few days to shoot around, get the rust off. Anytime after that. Okay if I use that table on the far side?"

The table I'd requested was the most distant from the coffee shop. The younger players didn't get over there much.

"You're going to attract a lot of bees."

"You know I don't talk when I play. They'll go away."

"Don't count on it, the way you're looking these days."

"That's nice of you to say," I said. "How's the wife?"

I'd forgotten what a pleasant laugh Andy had.

We stood up.

"That table number is twelve. I'll give you the reduced day rate and reserve it for you for three days, starting tomorrow. Today's free. Nice to have you back in town."

I shot around until the pool hall closed that evening, and when the young men who came by realized I wasn't going to speak to them, they wandered away as I thought they would.

The next day after breakfast I walked into the pool hall from the coffee shop and had most of the day to myself before the airmen got off duty and discovered that I'd returned. So, I put away my cue, caught a movie, had supper at a Mexican café, and got to bed early.

The day after that I followed a similar routine at the pool hall. When the airmen began to arrive, I quit my practice and decided to take a drive to relax.

I found Andy gluing tips.

"The other night, driving in, I saw a roadhouse near a truck stop."

"Barlow's," Andy said.

"Is that the place? They had a full parking lot, which usually indicates a decent kitchen."

"Prime rib's their specialty. They do a good job with it," he said.

"Feel like a supper break? I'm buying if you care to join me."

"Too busy, Baby. Try me again, though."

33

BARLOW'S WAS FARTHER out than I'd remembered, but the setting sun made the sky colorful and the evening was warm and dry, so the drive was pleasant.

I backed into a parking space over on the edge of the gravel lot. It was a long walk to the front door, but if I needed the car in a hurry, it would be easy to find and quick to the highway.

I locked up and started for the roadhouse. I'd been on my feet all day and looked forward to sitting down to a hot meal.

It's hard to say what makes one car stand out from another, especially in this part of the country where the big cars and pickup trucks all sported the same thick coating of dust and grime, but a particular car caught my attention. It was a late model Cadillac Coupe de Ville, two door.

Maybe it was the measured pace as it drifted between the parked cars. Its lights were not going to find me, but I stepped closer to a big pickup to make certain. And then I realized there was something I'd noticed. I'd recognized something about the driver, but what?

The Caddy rounded the end of the row and found a space one over. I moved to another spot so I could watch and not be seen. I felt foolish. I wasn't certain that I had seen anything, nothing definitive that's for sure, and yet—

A family had parked nearby and they'd all noticed me as they piled out and walked past. So convinced were they that I was spying on someone, they all turned their heads the direction that had my interest. I laughed at myself, but I continued watching until Spider Jack Tooley's lanky figure rose up from among the cars.

My nerves went twitchy.

Moments later Ugly joined Spider Jack and they walked off toward Barlow's.

I didn't know who I thought I was going to see, but even though I was surprised, in my heart I knew I shouldn't have been. Those two murderers worked for Travis Horner, and one of the cities from which he operated was Amarillo.

Okay. I knew who they were and where they were, but what was I going to do about it? Otis would say, here were two guys who needed killing.

And I'd agree with him.

Let's say I chose to do that. How would I go about it? A sawed-off shotgun at their car when they came out? Efficient, but obvious premeditation with two dozen witnesses, including the family that saw me spying.

It had to be done somewhere else, in privacy. Just the three of us: two cold-blooded killers and me.

Or, should that be three cold-blooded killers? Devil takes the hindmost.

What was I doing?

Look how easy it had been to discuss with myself

murdering Travis Horner and his hired killer when they were in Savannah's apartment. I was willing to ambush them and justify it because they were killers themselves. I knew I could walk away from that with a clear conscience and a better than even chance of getting away with it.

That was the issue, wasn't it? It wasn't should I kill them? It was if I killed them could I get away with it? I was beginning to think Lee and Lieutenant Lynch were on to something about me.

I was getting nowhere with all the introspection.

I retired to my car and sat staring across Barlow's parking lot. I was teetering on the edge. I was premeditating a double homicide.

Okay, instead of that, I could go to the Amarillo police, put them in touch with Lieutenant Lynch in Fort Worth, have him confirm Spider Jack Tooley's status as a fugitive, and let them do their job.

Except, I had read Travis' black book. A big shot at the Amarillo Police Department was on Travis' payroll, and these guys work for Travis.

Finally, I went inside.

I watched them from across the room and kept my mind open for a great idea to come to me. Before they finished their supper, I went back and gave my friend a call.

"Henry. What's happening?"

"Jim get out truck, find way into hospital, come to Otis room. Make nurses pull hair."

"My god. How'd he do all that?"

"I tell nurse lucky Jim not bring dead possum."

"Did he go back to the truck like a good boy?"

"Nurse say if happen again, she call police."

The sudden pressure on my neck was so intense my eyes rolled back. I was passing out.

Spider Jack Tooley's face was next to mine. He released the pressure some.

"You're Otis Millett's bitch, ain'tcha?"

He gripped my neck again so hard my knees felt wobbly.

"That hurts, don't it? You want some more, fuck with me. You'll get more."

We were in a hallway near the restrooms, but the dangling receiver and passing customers didn't concern him. He was rough and fast as he stripped me of the .38 under my arm and the .32 in my boot, and then he slapped me so hard my head snapped back like it was on a spring.

He slammed me out a side entrance. Blood from my nose was running into my mouth and over my chin. My heart was racing.

I was stumbling across the parking lot beside the big man before I knew clearly what was happening. His hands were strong; his grip on my neck was vise-like. He gave me another hard slap, shoved me into the back seat of their big car, and we were in motion.

"People saw us," Ugly said.

"They don't know what they saw," Spider Jack said. "Get our asses outta here, we don't gotta worry about it."

My ear was ringing from the last slap as I got off the floor and into the back seat. Ugly was putting on the steam, throwing gravel, as he steered the powerful car onto the highway, heading east on 66. He was pushing a hundred in seconds.

My neck and face ached. I pinched my nose to stanch the bleeding and worked my jaw. He hadn't broken anything, but there was no guarantee he wouldn't the next time he hit me. I didn't kid myself. Getting something broken by Spider Jack was the least of my worries.

But he'd helped me make up my mind. I was going to kill him. I was certain of it now.

As if he knew I was thinking about him, he turned and looked back at me. "Otis' bitch. This is nice, ain't it, Arbus? Otis' bitch." He pushed in the lighter and chuckled like he'd heard a good one as he shook out a cigarette.

Arbus said, "We oughta fill up before we go out to the warehouse."

"So, fill up."

"We was gonna do that at the truck stop."

"Okay. We didn't. There's a station before the turnoff."

"What about her? They'll see her."

"We'll throw her in the trunk."

"We got stuff back there, Jack. I don't want her in there."

"I'll knock her silly first."

"She could wake up and we wouldn't know."

Spider Jack moaned under his breath. "You got a blanket back there, ain'tcha? Some rope? We'll leave her where she's at." He turned and looked me in the eye. "You'll be a good little bitch, won'tcha?"

Spider Jack continued staring at me as Arbus pulled onto the shoulder and stopped.

Highway traffic was roaring past a dozen feet from us, rocking the car with repeated blasts of dry, hot air. On the distant horizon were the hundreds of tiny lights that defined a massive grain elevator, a Martian outpost in an Asimov story.

When Arbus got out and walked around to the trunk,

Spider Jack got out on his side and threw his seat forward. He sported his toothy grin and took his time as he leaned into the back and began grabbing for me. I thought of men I'd seen baiting a bear in a cage, laughing and poking it with sticks.

I restrained myself from kicking in his face. Even if I'd won the battle with Spider Jack, Arbus, who was peering through the window, would've shot me. Also, I didn't want to call attention to my boots. I had blades there and when the time was right—

"Come here," Spider Jack said, and finally got my leg in his tight grip and dragged me to him.

34

I DIDN'T KNOW how long I'd been unconscious.

My first impression was the hot, suffocating closeness of the wool blanket I was under. I was soaked with sweat and had a headache from hell. My face hurt from being hit. My hands stung; my fingers felt prickly.

The car wasn't moving. I listened for sounds of any kind. I was alone.

It was difficult to move with my arms tied behind my back. But my legs were free, so I was able to change position and worm my throbbing head from beneath the blanket. I wiggled my fingers and clenched my fists to get the feeling back to my blood-starved hands as I squirmed to a sitting position and looked outside.

They had parked the Coupe de Ville on the far edge of a well-lighted area where men were bringing cases of liquor from a warehouse and loading them into trucks identified as belonging to a furniture store.

I didn't know how much time I had, so I started at once solving the problem of getting a blade from my boot. I couldn't make a mistake with knives as sharp as those I carried, but that was academic if I couldn't even reach them. It took a moment, but I got an idea.

I wedged a boot beneath the front seat and used my other foot to pry it off. It took longer than I expected to get that done, but I finally got it accomplished. Once the boot was loose on the floor, I had to get on my back above it to get it in my hands. Then it was a scramble to get back on the seat keeping the boot behind me.

During the retrieval I'd lost my view out the window. I didn't know until my head was up again if the situation had changed.

It had.

There were now a half dozen men standing near the big open warehouse doors. They were talking and smoking. Spider Jack and Arbus were among them.

I worked as quickly as I could, knowing a false move could cause me to slice a wrist beyond any hope of survival. I got the blade positioned and began the agitation that would move the blade through the rope.

After a moment, I felt the warmth of blood. I'd nicked myself.

With steel that sharp, there'd been no feeling of having been cut, and I had no idea how badly I was cut, either.

I kept moving. Easy. Easy.

Just as the men ended their talk and began walking away, the rope gave. The blade had gone through it. My hands were free.

Spider Jack looked irritated. Arbus had to hustle along to keep up with his long strides. They'd parked so far away they were still a few moments from the car.

Good. I needed those moments to get done everything I needed to do.

I was back under the blanket before they got there.

When Spider Jack got in, he slammed his door hard, and he started in on Arbus the instant he entered from the other side.

"I'm sick of hearin' about her fuckin' suitcase," Spider Jack said.

"We never seen it," Arbus said, and fired up the Cadillac.

"You're damned right. That's the first thing. We never seen the fuckin' thing."

I felt the difference in the ride as the car left the warehouse area and picked up speed on a gravel road.

"He can't control that hillbilly bitch and now we're back in it," Spider said.

"How we gonna do it, Spider?"

"Pick up Savannah again, you mean?"

"Yeah. How're we supposed to get her away from her home?"

"Shoot that old one-eyed bastard and his whole fuckin' family. That's how."

"I don't know, Jack."

"Travis said don't come back without her."

"I know, but come on, Jack. You think we ain't gonna stick out over in them Ozark Mountains?"

"You're right. We ain't hillbillies."

"They're gunnin' for us, too," Arbus said. "Our welcome is wore out in Oklahoma."

"And we never even seen that fuckin' suitcase," Spider Jack said.

There was a long pause, and then Arbus said, "What about her?"

"Who?" Spider Jack asked.

"Her," Arbus said.

"Fuck! I forgot all about Otis' bitch."

I grew tense. I liked it better when I wasn't the subject.

"Maybe we shoulda told Travis," Arbus said.

"He woulda just took her for hisself, Arbus, What's wrong with you?"

"What if he finds out?"

"There ain't nobody gonna find out. There's a place I been to huntin' rabbit. Just north of here a little. I'll show you. It was a Indian place way back. Has a dry well. We can do her out there and get rid of her when we're finished. Nobody but Indian spirits'll know. Just another missin' girl."

"I don't know," Arbus said.

"I know. Stop worryin'," Spider Jack said, "and slow down. The turnoff's just up here."

It was directions left and right on desolate prairie roads after that until Spider Jack said they'd reached the old Indian homestead.

"You're right," Arbus said. "Nobody'd ever find this place."

"Park over there," Spider Jack said. "Close to the well."

The big car rolled to a stop and Arbus cut the engine.

The blanket was snatched off me and I was looking at Spider Jack staring at me over the front seat. Arbus set the emergency brake, and then he, too, turned to look over his shoulder at me.

In the distance I heard the yips of coyotes as my heart tripped against my ribcage. I was curled up on my side with my hands behind me. In each hand was a blade. I swung my legs to the floor and sat up, keeping to the center of the back seat.

"Look at this, Arbus. The bitch is wide awake."

"Uh huh," Arbus mumbled, staring at me.

"We'll have to cut her outta them jeans," Spider Jack said.

I'd been massaging the knife handles to keep the blood circulating in my hands and arms. When I moved, I'd have to move fast.

"Remember that bitch over in Tucson?" Spider Jack asked Arbus. "Her fancy underwear…"

"She screamed so much," Arbus said in a voice so soft and joyful I thought he might laugh.

"Maybe this one's a screamer," Spider Jack whispered.

I said, "You believe in Indian spirits, Jack?"

They were shocked. Their faces froze.

I assumed they expected crying, begging, screaming. They hadn't expected me to speak in a calm voice.

Spider Jack was the first to surface from their heinous fantasy.

"What kinda question is that, you dumb bitch?"

"How about you, Arbus. Believe in ghosts?"

Arbus squinted. He didn't like the subject.

"I see ghosts out there." I nodded my head toward the windshield and Arbus and Spider Jack both looked.

I moved instantly, swinging my hands out as I fell forward, chopping my blades into their necks as if I were striking cymbals. The first cuts were to the bone, but I slashed up and pressed in, doing even more injury as I withdrew, leaving their neck wounds open wide and their heads nearly detached from their bodies.

As blood erupted from severed arteries spraying the dash and front window, their damaged throats didn't allow them human sounds. Spider Jack's arm briefly flopped like a headless chicken, then the killers buckled forward and were dead within seconds of the attack.

This is the way the world ends.

I exhaled. I'd been holding my breath.

I was numb and unwilling to move. I'd won, but somehow I didn't feel like a winner. My heart pounded as I listened. For what? The battle yelp of Comanche warriors? But there was nothing to hear after the spewing and gurgling was finished in the front seat, nothing save the soft sounds of a warm prairie night.

I went out a back window, got the car keys, and opened the trunk. I found some tape and bandages and wrapped my arm where I'd cut myself. After that, I surveyed the challenge of getting the dead guys out of the car. The amount of blood was incredible, and it was everywhere.

I had to avoid getting smeared with blood. I was a long way from home and I didn't want to have to explain anything to anyone. I found a shirt that fit me like a tent and some gloves in the trunk and put them on before pulling the bloodied killers out, one to each side of the car. I cleaned their pockets of weapons, personal items, and money. Everything got tossed into the front seat except the money. I'd spend that.

Next, I stepped away from the car and the carnage and cleaned my blades using a towel I found in the trunk. Busy work. I needed the time to calm down, clear my head.

I finally stopped moving.

I went over, gazed down at Spider Jack's remains, and said, "This girl didn't go missing, did she?" And like an answer to my question came the rasp and chatter of a nearby ground owl.

I contemplated dragging the Einsteins over to the well and tossing them in, but decided against it. That was too much like a burial, something neither of them deserved.

What was correct, I wondered, considering how they'd treated the girl in Tucson and who knows how many others and the way they would've treated me—before and after they'd killed me?

That helped me with my decision.

I left them where the coyotes could feed on them and called it a night.

35

HENRY HAD TAUGHT me to read the night sky.

"North of here," Spider Jack had said.

By keeping the Cadillac on a southward course, I located Route 66. When I was a couple of miles from the highway, I pulled over and shut off the car.

The dashboard clock said it had been just less than three hours since Spider Jack had invited me to join them for a ride.

I'd used several wool blankets to cover the seat and had wiped down the steering wheel as best I could to make the bloody machine drivable, but this was the end of the road for the Coupe de Ville.

The trunk contained ample proof of Arbus' cautious nature. It had all types of emergency supplies, including a gallon tin of gasoline. I poured the gasoline over the car interior, threw a fiery matchbook in, and walked away, glad to be rid of the heavy, rusty smell of blood.

It took less time than I'd thought it would to snare a big rig.

My manicure was paying off.

As I climbed into the air-conditioned cab, I glanced

back at the flames. From that distance they seemed no more than a campfire.

"Thanks for stopping," I said, and gave the trucker the sweetest smile I could conjure up. "You're a lifesaver."

"This call is long distance," I cautioned Henry.

I was using the same phone I'd used when Spider Jack interrupted my earlier call. From the moment Henry answered, it had been a nonstop lecture about how worried he was and how I had to start taking care of myself.

"You think long distance cost important issue? No wonder Jim act crazy. Look his mama."

I had to smile at that one.

"Finish telling me how that big dog got up to Otis' room," I said.

Henry took obvious relish in describing how pleased with himself Jim had been when he found Otis' room at the hospital, wagging his big tail, knocking instruments about, and ducking under the bed to get away from the nurses.

And how happy it had made Otis to have something exciting happening around him.

"Otis tell nurse if food not get better, Jim come back every day."

"When can Otis go home?"

"Doctor lift eyebrows. Never say. Nurse say she think two week, maybe."

"He's going to be all right, isn't he, Henry? He's going to be our Otis. This is not going to change him."

"Bullets go bad places. Take time heal. How long you gone?"

"I'll be home soon. I got a couple of things out of the

way this evening. With a little luck, a plan I have going will take care of the rest of our problem."

"At kitchen table you talk more straight from shoulder."

Straight from shoulder?

"Tell Jim I'm proud of him," I said. "I'll call tomorrow."

When Henry said, "Goodnight, Baby Girl," I felt like crying.

Could I be anyone's baby girl and do the things I did?

In my heart, I knew the world was better off without sick bastards like Spider Jack and the men who tried to kill me at the office. And what was I supposed to do if they came after me? I'd sworn long ago never to be a victim again.

I left Barlow's by the side entrance and walked directly to my car, tears flowing. I don't know how long I sat in my car and cried.

"I've had enough. I've had enough," I said and cried until I couldn't cry anymore.

Teresa Brewer was singing when I arrived at Andy's late the next morning. I knew the jukebox rotation. Frankie Laine was next.

I said hello to Ginny at the coffee counter and ordered a Dr Pepper and some fries. I started to tell her where I'd be, but she said, "Table twelve," and smiled.

See? A pleasant attitude and a good tip worked wonders.

There were a few other early birds at the tables as I crossed the poolroom. Here and there were the sounds of striking billiard balls. I adored the crack of billiard balls and the gulp of the pockets; no other sounds were remotely similar.

I put my case on one of the chairs near table twelve, removed a stick, assembled it, and placed it on the tabletop. After closing my case and putting it behind the chair against the wall, I chalked my cue.

I set it aside again as Ginny arrived with pop, a glass of ice, and fries with a fork so I could keep my fingers clean.

I don't believe the waitresses had ever seen anyone practice all day the way I'd done the past few days. Ginny, in particular, sometimes stood for a while watching as I worked a corner shot until I was satisfied.

That morning she said, "I didn't know girls shot pool until you showed up."

"Girls can do whatever they want," I told her.

"It's arranged," Andy said as he walked up and Ginny got back to work.

"Good," I said.

"Breakfast of champions?" he asked me when he saw my pop and fries.

I smiled. Andy had children at home.

He hiked his brow and got back on the subject. "I tried to set it for this coming Saturday, but when he heard it was Baby Shark looking to play him, tomorrow night was as far away as he would agree to."

"So he's heard of me."

He nodded. "And he thinks your reputation is overblown."

"Perfect," I said. "Did he agree to a bill a game and five a match?"

"He did, and he would've agreed to more, he's so

puffed up. You want to shoot around some on the table you'll be using?"

"Nah. That's nice of you, but I don't need an edge. In fact, I'm going to shut it down right now until tomorrow. It's such a pretty day, I think I'll take a swim and get some sun. What time tomorrow?"

"Eight sharp," Andy said.

I telephoned the Smikes in Oklahoma.

Bronagh was mourning the loss of her son Eustace and was full of hate and thoughts of revenge. I tried not to fuel her rage as I expressed my sympathy.

I gave her my number at the motel and left a message for Buford.

He phoned me an hour or so later. Dolores called me away from poolside.

I told him, "I know where Travis Horner will be tomorrow night for a couple of hours starting at eight o'clock."

"You're sure about that?"

"Positive," I said. "He'll be with me."

It was all about details after that.

When I hung up, I returned to the swimming pool confident that things were going in the right direction.

The next day I had lunch with Dolores at a restaurant near the Methodist church where she attended services. Very civilized. Soups and salads. Women in white gloves. I was an oddity, but I got a sweet smile from every lady I caught staring at me.

"What does your mama think about you shootin' pool?" Dolores asked me over her salad.

"She died before I took up the game," I said.

"You were how old?"

"Sixteen."

"You weren't much older than that when Harlan brought you through here the first time."

"I was eighteen. It was August and hot as I recall."

"You wouldn't stay out of the swimming pool and I couldn't keep the boys away. There was hardly any room for my guests with all the Air Force boys sneaking in."

"I remember you yelling at them."

"Oh, I'm sure I was awful. Manfred was still driving for that farm equipment outfit and gone all the time and Harlan was no help. He let you do pretty much what you wanted."

"I was always a good girl."

"That you were, dear. I never saw one better."

36

WHEN WE GOT back to the motel, I called Henry's number. But I didn't get an answer. I knew it was a long shot trying to catch Henry in the middle of the day. He was away from the house working, and later he'd be at the hospital with Otis.

I was getting antsy. I'd be finished in Amarillo tonight and on my way home soon after. My concern about how things were going at home was going to have to wait.

I stared at the walls for a while. It's not enough what life throws at us, there's always family, too.

I decided to take a nap.

That evening when I was getting dressed, what I saw in the mirror made me happy that I'd spent some time in the sun. A good tan always brings out the blue of my eyes. The bruising on my face was a thing of the past, and Dolores' hairdresser had done a nice trim on my hair. Even my manicure had survived the workout from the other evening.

Shined boots, new black jeans that were a perfect fit,

and a fresh cotton shirt the color of ripe peaches topped it off. I was ready.

At ten minutes after eight, I pulled into the parking lot at Andy's. I arrived late to piss off Travis and to guarantee an entrance.

The smoke-filled pool hall was busier than usual and went quiet just the way I wanted it to when it became known that I'd arrived. I had the entire room to cross, since we were playing at the special table in back. I saw Andy there with Travis by his side, but the owner moved away at once to come meet me.

Local men who'd heard about the contest matched the young airmen in number. Here and there an airman applauded until all the young men got their nerve up and the place broke into clamor and applause.

"You've got 'em all excited, Baby. I should've sold tickets," the owner said as he walked up wearing a wide grin. "You want me to get that?" He indicated my cue case.

"Nah, thanks, Andy. I like having it in my hand."

"Okay by me," he said, and led me off through the tables and the boisterous young men that lined our way.

Looking at the faces, I realized I missed the hustling days. The way men moved away as I drew closer, as if there were some magic to my presence, some mystery to my skill at the table, something about me that demanded caution.

Once the crowd noise had begun, it didn't cease until we'd arrived at the table and Andy raised his hands. "I'm glad you could all be here this evening. You're going to see some astounding pool. A reminder: no noise, please, during play."

The place went silent as I put my cue case aside and Andy turned to Travis and said, "Travis Horner, allow me to introduce Kristin Van Dijk, Baby Shark."

Travis stepped forward with an extended hand. He was wearing a light gray wool suit, dark blue silk tie, and had an arrogant smirk on his face. I shook his hand.

He kept his voice down. "What shall I call you? Baby Shark feels a bit awkward."

"You'll get used to it," I said.

"You're Otis Millett's partner, aren't you?" he asked. I didn't answer him.

"How's he doing? I understand he had an accident."

He was messing with me, but he was an amateur. Wait until I *accidentally* messed with him.

Andy spoke to us, but loudly enough for all to hear. "I'm referee and scorekeeper. The standard rules of nine ball apply. I'll call bad hits and fouls and mine is the last word." He held up a large white card. "Frames and matches won will be noted below the players' names here so everyone can see it. We'll lag for first break and alternate after that. A race to five games wins a match, and then a new match begins."

He spoke more quietly to us. "We'll start when you're ready."

I enjoyed the idea of making Travis wait, so I took my time choosing a stick, putting it together, and getting it chalked. I had that time to glance around and recognize a face here and there. I nodded at the guys I knew. They liked being recognized.

There were a few young women. Ginny was among them. I smiled at her and she blushed as her friends began plying her with questions.

When I stepped around to the end of the table, Andy

provided the cue balls, and Travis and I lagged. I won, but it was close. It looked as if he knew how to control his shot. That was good.

I'd hoped that Travis would shoot a decent game. I needed distraction from wanting to attack him for the injury that he'd inflicted on Otis and the attempts on my life and the sorrow that he had created for the Smike family.

After all the suggestions that had been made to me to seek psychiatric analysis, I had to wonder if anyone had ever suggested to Travis Horner that he should speak to a professional?

Uh huh.

I chalked again as Andy racked the balls for nine ball: number one on the foot spot to be struck first, number nine protected in the middle, number eight in last position, all balls touching in a perfect diamond shape.

I saw Dapper Dan standing among the crowd looking smart in a suit and tie. It seems Savannah missed him as well as Travis when she fired at them the other night. He was younger and smaller than the other two thugs I spied as Travis employees.

A driver and two bodyguards was how I read it.

I sank a ball on the break and a couple of shots later put the nine ball in the corner. Nine ball is a fast game and good players can speed through several frames before you know it. Travis had won three games when I won game five and ended the first match.

The purpose behind my play was to keep Travis at the pool hall for an hour or two. My strategy was to allow him to win as many games as possible without allowing him a match. I wanted him to believe he could beat me so he would continue to play—I was, in effect, hustling him under the guise of a contest.

He was at a disadvantage that particular evening because I had what players call a dead stroke going; I was shooting flawlessly.

It was as if I couldn't miss, and the crowd reacted to the better plays. Travis didn't like losing, but his stroke wasn't getting any better. And since he was a bully and accustomed to taking by force what he couldn't obtain through talent or skill, it was especially difficult for him to keep getting so close to winning.

After taking a game or two on his hopeful way to five to win a match, he had an annoying habit of smacking his lips with satisfaction and glancing about for crowd reaction. What he should've been doing was chalking his cue. The miscues that cost him so dearly were almost all due to his forgetting that simple task.

When I thought I'd kept him at Andy's long enough, I timed an accident.

I was chalking my cue as Travis moved around the end of the table, his eyes on his next shot. I turned as if I didn't see him and punched the toe of my boot directly into his ankle.

He cried out.

I followed through like I was catching my balance, stepped on the bridge of his injured foot, and gave him a shove.

He cried out again, staggered back, lost his footing, and fell to the floor. I didn't see an ounce of pretense in his response. The man was suffering.

Good.

No one seemed certain what was happening. Andy

and one of Travis' bodyguards got to him first. There was confusion. What happened? Did he want to be helped up from the floor? Did he need a doctor?

I kept my distance as Andy and Travis' men worked out what to do.

The crowd pushed forward and, as usual, there were many points of view and even more opinions. However, it was generally agreed that Travis and I had accidentally collided.

Travis didn't think he could stand. It was decided to help him into a chair. When he finally met my gaze, I smiled. I wanted to confirm any suspicion he might've had that I'd kicked his ankle on purpose.

After a few more minutes of discussion, Andy came over to me.

"He said you ran into him. He thinks it was intentional."

"He's confused, Andy. It was an accident, but so what? Where do we go from here?"

"He needs a little time to see if he's able to go on. He's recovering from a broken ankle and he's not certain how this collision with you is going to leave him."

"I'm sorry to hear that," I said. "He was just starting to get his stroke."

Andy rolled his eyes. "He hasn't won a match in an hour and a half. Let's take a break. If he's not ready to play in twenty minutes or so, we'll call it quits. Okay?"

37

DAPPER DAN WAS outside the ladies room door waiting to speak to me. We were in a short hall, a cul-de-sac, out of sight from the poolroom. I paused and looked him in the eye. We were close to the same height.

"Travis has a message for you."

"He couldn't hobble over with it himself?" I said.

"I'd watch that smart mouth, if I was you."

"If you were me, you'd be taller," I told him.

A woman came from the room and I exchanged smiles with her as she passed.

"So what's the message, Dan?"

He didn't know why I'd called him Dan, but he said, "Travis said to tell you that little kick of yours was a mistake you'd regret."

I hit Dan in the face with an open-handed slap. I brought it from the basement, fast and hard. He hadn't expected it, didn't see it coming, and stepped back from the power of it.

"That's my reply," I said.

Dan had the reflexes of a sloth. He blinked several

times. His face grew red, and then he actually moved to hit me back.

I stepped inside his swing, ducked down, and delivered a solid right uppercut to his groin. I'd seen a prelim lightweight in a four rounder do that with the referee on the other side of the fighter he'd hit. The ref missed it, but the crowd went nuts

Dan had no crowd on his side. I got away with it.

He gasped for air. When I saw he was losing strength in his knees, I grabbed him by his stylish suit lapel and dragged him into the ladies' room, where he collapsed to his knees and retched.

I took my .38 from my purse and pistol-whipped him across the back of his head. That blow knocked him unconscious and sent him face first to the tile floor.

"I react badly to threats, Dan."

It didn't take long to locate Ginny standing with her friends.

"I wonder if I can ask a favor?" I said to her when I walked up.

"What do you need?" she said, all business.

"Some drunk has stumbled into the ladies' room and passed out."

"Oh, no," she said.

"He's made kind of a mess and I didn't want to bother Andy with it. Maybe you could get a couple of the guys from the kitchen to drag him out of there and throw him into the alley out back."

Ginny was moving away as she said, "I'll see to it."

Ginny's young women friends had heard everything and all made appropriate faces of disapproval.

"Guys can be such pigs," one of them said.

When I returned to the table, Andy told me Travis was

unable to continue playing because of his ankle injury. He said that I was the undisputed winner. Travis had taken some games, but he hadn't won any matches.

Andy said, "He's saying that his ankle kept him from playing at his best, but I don't think anyone here believes that."

"As long as he brings money, he can have a rematch," I said.

"Speaking of money," Andy said. "Stick around and I'll settle with you before you leave."

Andy announced to the crowd that the match was concluded and that Baby Shark had won. Everyone already knew that, so the reaction was tepid. He held up the white card on which he'd kept the score, but no one paid any attention. The show was over, it was a weeknight, and the crowd was heading for home. There had been some side bets and as those got settled, the bettors left, too.

Several men and almost all the women came by to congratulate me on their way out.

Travis raised his voice about wanting to leave, but no one seemed to know where his driver was. I didn't think anyone would look in the alley near the garbage cans.

Travis finally left without Dapper Dan. The assumption was at least one of the two bull-necked bodyguards knew how to drive. Travis didn't bother to even glance my way as he limped out with the assistance of one of his goons.

An ignominious ending, my dad would've said.

Andy was a businessman and had everything ready to go. The game had made us money; his food and beer had sold well, so he was happy.

"You're driving back in the morning?"

"Early," I said.

"Straight through, or are you hustling your way back?"

"Straight through," I said. "I should be home by noon."

"Well, drive carefully, Baby, and come back anytime. You're always welcome at the Snooker Palace."

Whatever traffic the pool hall crowd had created, it was long gone by the time I got on the road to Dolores'. And I thought they rolled up the sidewalks early in Fort Worth.

I had the windows down. The night was warm and dry and carried the scent of cattle from the train yards. I was looking forward to a swim at the motel and a good night's sleep.

During the summers, I used to like taking a dip in the big cement tank below the windmill at Henry's. The nights would be so hot and the water so cold. Sometimes I could talk Jim into jumping in, but he was a big sissy about it and needed a lot of help getting out until Henry built him some steps and a platform where he could stand and bark.

Up ahead I saw a police car over on the wide shoulder of the road, its colored lights blinking. It was parked near a Cadillac sedan that had all its lights shining, inside and out, and all four doors open wide.

I slowed down as I passed and heard the squawk of the police radio. The two men that had been shot dead in the front seat were Travis' goons. There was damage to the windshield, door, and roof—shotguns.

There was no sign of Travis.

The policeman was walking around the Cadillac and looking inside. In my rearview mirror I saw another police car coming.

I couldn't've been more than thirty or forty minutes behind Travis. What had happened beside the road out there had just happened. Whoever shot those guys didn't have a big head start. Though the policeman at the scene probably didn't know that.

I guessed if the shooters had been going east, they'd be pretty close to the Oklahoma border in another hour. Of course, the shooters might've gone any direction. Who was to say where the police should look?

But let's say, just for argument's sake, the shooters went east. The police couldn't stop every car on Route 66, even if they knew who they were looking for, which they didn't, I guessed.

I drove on, leaving the crime scene behind me.

I thought about lucky Dapper Dan. He'd survived that evening by being a no-show when it was time to leave with Travis Horner. He'd avoided harm that night at Savannah's apartment, too. He seemed to have a charmed life.

"How fortunate for him," I said to myself. "And how nice the Smikes and Travis Horner are together at last."

38

OVER COFFEE AND breakfast rolls the next morning, Dolores quoted from the morning paper and filled me in about the shooting on the highway.

"The men who were shot were bodyguards," she said. "Were they at Andy's with that disgusting Travis Horner?"

"They may have been," I said.

"You didn't see them?"

"It was pretty crowded."

"They think Horner was in the car, but there wasn't any sign of him when the police arrived."

"Oh yeah?"

"They're looking for him. They're thinking it was a kidnapping."

"Incredible," I said. "This happened just down the road from here. You be careful, Dolores. There are crazies out there."

"We know that, don't we, Greta?"

Greta emitted a tiny squeak as she arched her back and yawned.

The drive home from Amarillo took about five hours. The route angled down from the heart of the high plains, skimmed along the southwestern edge of Oklahoma into Wichita Falls, and then dropped from there to Fort Worth.

I was carrying my things up the back stairs to my apartment by one o'clock.

I didn't want to go to the hospital until I'd stopped by to see how things were at the office. Henry said Otis was sounding like his old self, so I knew he'd want to hear about everything.

It was unusual for Madame Li to follow me upstairs, but she wanted to talk. At first she just wanted to make sure I was satisfied with the paint and repairs. She chatted as she walked around checking things.

She finally got to the real reason she'd come up when she told me she'd been by several times to visit Otis.

"He walks with a cane," she said. "You know how he is, though. He says not for long."

"I wasn't aware he was up and walking," I said.

"For two days now."

"Henry hasn't said anything."

"Well, then they want to surprise you. Don't you imagine?"

"Knowing those two, that's believable."

"Pretend you're surprised," Madame Li suggested.

"That'll make them happy," I said.

"And how are you, Miss Van Dijk?"

"How do you mean?"

"The bruising on your face is gone, but have you fully recovered from that awful attack?"

"I believe so, yes, thank you."

"I found myself unable to sleep for several nights and

I only experienced the aftermath of what you physically suffered."

"I'm sorry, Madame. I hadn't meant for you to see anything."

"Of course not."

"I called you the night it happened because I didn't want you to be taken by surprise and frightened the next morning."

"I understand that." She paused, but I knew she wasn't finished. "You and Otis must sometimes see what police officers see in their line of work," she said.

"Not often, but sometimes we do."

"It would no doubt harden one to some degree," she said.

Please don't suggest I speak to a psychiatrist.

"We try to keep things in perspective," I said.

She nodded. "Otis is firm. His work demands it, but he's also compassionate."

"Mmmm," I hummed, wondering where this was going.

She said, "I've been concerned about Otis."

She paused again. I waited.

Without looking at me, which was not her usual manner, she said, "I'm quite fond of him, as you must know."

"He's fond of you, as well," I said, and wished at once that I'd held my tongue.

She gazed at me directly and said, "Is he?"

I replied sincerely, "I've never heard him say anything that would discourage that opinion," but it was as if I were quoting from a nineteenth century novel.

This wasn't my kind of conversation.

After a long moment, noted for its silence, we discussed

the leather sofa. While I was gone, the upholsterer had returned it.

"It cleaned up nicely," I said, and we expressed our pleasure about that.

Before she went back downstairs, she made me promise to stop for a bowl of soup and hot tea on my way out. It was an easy promise. I hadn't eaten since rolls and coffee with Dolores in Amarillo.

Madame Li.

I had to smile. Given her breeding, her education, her sense of fashion—Otis had to be her bad boy, didn't he?

I turned on the old floor fan, sat at the big desk, and called Lee's number at work. He was in the field. I left a message to let him know I was back.

Henry was right about my relationship with Lee. I was going to have to be strong, take control of my life. I loved Lee, but breaking up was the best thing for us.

Or at least I thought it was.

I was what Otis would call more messed up than nine bulldogs.

The way I understood it, it was either end my relationship with Lee or change the direction of my life, not that the direction of my life was anything to brag about. But being a private investigator was all I knew, and I thought, overall, I was doing some good. Also, every year I got better at it.

I jumped when the phone rang.

It was Lee. My heart turned over.

"I'm running right now, but I wanted to check in," he said.

"I won't keep you," I said. "I just wanted you to know I was back in town."

"Have a late supper with me, Kristin. Okay? Let's go out to *Puerto Perdido,* have a few beers, and do some dancing. It's been too long since we've done that."

I couldn't catch my breath for a moment. He was suggesting the restaurant where we'd had our first date, our first dance, where he'd first kissed me.

I heard his partner telling him to hurry up.

"I'll meet you at the hospital later. Wear your dancing shoes, shorty."

He hung up.

It seemed forever since he'd called me shorty.

I sat there shaking my head. What was that business about taking control of my life? I wasn't in control of anything. If there was anyone in this life being swept along by the whims of circumstance, it was yours truly.

I phoned our answering service.

We had six calls. Buford Smike had called twice; Andy in Amarillo; Sidecar Sanchez; and two from prospective clients. I made a list, but I couldn't bring myself to pick up the phone. I heaved a sigh, leaned back in the squeaky chair, and stared at the tin ceiling for a while.

I'd run out of personality.

I wanted to put off calling everyone back, but Otis' work ethic won out and I finally picked up the phone and dialed.

Buford's calls were to finalize the Travis Horner affair.

"The family is in your debt," he said.

"Let's be friends and call it even," I said.

Before he hung up, he said, "You haven't heard the last from me."

I had to admit his Ozark accent was certainly attractive.

Sidecar Sanchez just wanted an update on Otis' health. I was starting to like him.

Andy's call was interesting. He wanted to warn me that Travis' nephew had been asking about me.

"I didn't know he had a nephew," I said.

"Well, he does. I told him you were back home in Fort Worth before I realized I should be keeping quiet. I thought you should know about it."

"Thanks, Andy. No problem."

A nephew?

The two other calls were potential clients: a suspicious husband and a sister suspicious of her sister's husband. The last thing they wanted to do was talk to me on the phone. I told them Otis would call them back tomorrow, and hoped to myself I could arrange that.

I put my notes in my pocketbook, locked the office, and went downstairs for some lunch.

39

I ARRIVED AT the hospital bearing gifts, since our smitten landlady had insisted on me taking along some of Otis' favorites from her dinner menu. The nurses knew the packaging, word got around that Chinese cuisine had arrived, and I had plenty of help getting the food to Otis' room.

Madame Li had told me she was embarrassed to admit good fortune from Otis' grief, but the Mandarin Palace had gained customers from the hospital staff.

My partner wasn't in his room.

"He's been threatening to leave," a nurse advised me with her tongue jammed firmly in her cheek.

It was obvious they were all in on it when Otis came, well, strolling wouldn't be exactly right, but he was moving as casually as he could with the help of a stout and colorful, hand-carved cane from Mexico.

I couldn't've been happier if he'd been dancing a jig. To see him alive and so far along the road to recovery did me a world of good.

He stopped in the doorway and posed in his pajamas

and slippers and a gorgeous raw silk, ecru-colored robe, one I'd never seen before.

I smiled as wide as I could and said, "How handsome you are in your new robe, Mister Millett."

"I ain't so sure it's a compliment, but Madame Li said I looked like an ancient ivory statue."

Our Buddha had lost some poundage, however, but his next comment made it clear he saw his weight reduction as temporary.

"Let's head over to Sylvia's for a porterhouse and some of them pan fried potatoes, want to?"

"Just what you need," I said.

"It ain't the nurses' fault," he pointed out, "but the food here'd gag a buzzard."

"Why don't you get off your feet and we'll set you up with some Mandarin Palace chow."

The nurses agreed with me and moved at once to help him with that transition.

He gave me one of his faces and said, "You on the staff here now? Givin' orders and such."

"Oh, relax and get comfortable, big guy. We have a lot to talk about."

He grinned, and said, "You're right, Missy. I wanna hear what's been goin' on. It's like pullin' hen's teeth to get anything out of anybody around here."

Each of the nurses caught my eye to make certain I knew her job wasn't easy. I gave them return looks to say I understood, and together we got Otis back in bed.

"Crank this thing up, will you?" he said before he was properly settled.

"I knew there was a reason I hadn't taken up nursing," I said, and everyone in the room smiled except Otis.

I peered into the cartons of Chinese takeout, separated

the dishes I knew Otis would eat, and sent the balance of the generous offering away with the nurses.

When we were alone, Otis made my heart swell when he said, "I've missed you, Missy."

"Are you putting on a show to get out of here, or do you really feel as well as you're acting?"

"Some of each, I reckon. If I had my druthers, I wouldn't be here, but I know they need to keep their eye on me a while longer."

"Want to get caught up some?"

"Please, Missy. Give me something to think about besides being in this hospital."

"Travis Horner and a half dozen or so of his lieutenants, including Spider Jack Tooley, are roasting in hell. How's that?"

"You start with the good stuff. I'll say that for you. I'm gonna lean back and pretend I'm smoking a Lucky and you just give me a blow by blow account from the day I got shot right up till you walked in here this afternoon."

And that's what I did.

I figured Otis was as close as I was ever going to get to an analyst, so I did it up proud. I told him everything, just as if I'd written a book and he'd read it.

As the time passed, nurses floated through, performing their tasks, but we basically had the room to ourselves for a good long time. Otis was reclined in bed and I was in a chair near him.

When I was finished and asked him what he thought we should do with Travis' box of pictures and information, he said, "I don't think we wanna mess too much in Oklahoma politics, but I've heard about an honest young lawyer up there who's shaking things up... Cannon, I think his name is. They say he can talk a dog down from a meat truck. Maybe he'd be a good fella to end up with that box of goodies. Nobody knows that stuff is in our possession, right?"

"Just you and me. Well, and Henry, if he opened the package."

"Family," Otis said.

"Henry says that, too."

"Speaking of family, I helped Cooty and Edna with a down payment on a little house."

"I'm not surprised."

"He's working full time for Hank and says he'll pay me back. You oughta see that Millie. She comes by to throw up on me most every day."

Even if he were the right age, I had a hard time seeing Otis as a grandpa. But if squeezing that baby girl made him happy, who was I to say anything?

"The Smikes call regularly to ask about you."

"Do they know what happened to Spider Jack?"

"Only the two of us, Otis."

"Good. Silence can never come back to bite you, Missy."

"You know Madame Li is sweet on you, don't you?"

"You just findin' that out?"

"I always thought it was respect," I said.

We gazed at each other for a moment or so, neither of us wanting to deal with infatuation issues.

Otis looked past me.

"You probably have the wrong room," he said.

I looked over my shoulder and there was Dapper Dan standing in the doorway. He was decked out in a new suit and silk tie, a handsome young guy with a bruise on the left side of his face.

When I stood up and turned toward him, he stepped

into the room, and spoke to me. "You remember me, don't you?"

"You work for Travis Horner," I said.

"That's right."

"You're his driver. What can I do for you?"

"I'm more than his driver. Travis Horner's my uncle," he said.

Otis spoke up.

"That may be so, son, but you're in my room. What do you want?"

Dan looked past me as if he had just become aware of Otis. There was a kind of slowness about him that I had noticed before.

"You must be Otis Millett," he said.

"That's right. What can I do for you?"

"I'm looking for my uncle," Dan said. "He went missing last night."

"I'm sorry to hear that, but he's not here."

"She knows where my uncle is," he said.

"What're you talking about?" I said. "I read in an Amarillo paper this morning the police are looking for him. Have you spoken to them?"

"You're too clever by half," he said, and advanced into the room.

Otis pushed the button that summons a nurse as Dapper Dan strolled past the foot of the bed. He stepped into the only open space in the small room, stopped there, and turned fully toward us with a small revolver in his hand.

Everyone had a moment to catch a breath.

"You're makin' a mistake, son," Otis said.

"I don't think so," Dan said.

Otis said, "Put that away while you still can."

"I'm tired of being punched in the face. If it's not you hitting me, it's her."

"Nobody's going to hit you," I said.

"But somebody's likely to plug you if you keep waggin' that peashooter around," Otis said.

"I'll be on my way after you tell me where I can find my uncle."

I said, "The last time I saw your uncle was in the poolroom last night."

"Uncle Travis said you always have your nose where it doesn't belong."

"That's the truth," Otis said. "But that don't mean she knows where Travis is. Now put that piece away."

"I don't think so," Dan said. "I might have to shoot somebody."

Otis brought a .45 out from behind his pillow, leveled it at Dan, and took on another voice all together. "That kinda talk'll get you killed, boy."

"I'm not scared of you," Dan said. He took a step toward the bed and pointed his little pistol at Otis' face.

"Then you must be one of them kamikazes like in the Pacific campaign," my partner said.

Dan spoke to a nurse who had come to the doorway and was watching with wide eyes. "Close that door and go away."

The nurse closed the door.

It was eerie when Dan smiled. "She knew to do as she was told," he said.

At least he was still talking.

I said, "If you die here today, how does that help you find your uncle?"

"Maybe I won't die," he said.

"You will, son. I guarantee it," Otis said, "unless you holster your weapon."

"Don't press him, Otis. No mistakes."

"Maybe I'll shoot you between the eyes," Dan said. "That wouldn't be a mistake."

I walked around the end of the bed.

I heard Otis say my name as I moved between them, blocking the line of fire. I wanted the threat of death to stop. I needed a respite from mutilated bodies and blood.

"No one's going to get trigger happy," I said to Dan. "Not you and not Otis, because I'm going to apologize to you."

Dan gave me that eerie smile again and said, "What're you talking about?"

"You heard me. I'm sorry I hit you. I'm sorry I treated you the way I did." I stared into Dan's eyes. I made him look at me. "Did you hear me?"

He nodded his head yes and said, "I'm done talking. Where's my Uncle Travis?"

It was plain to see the slow-thinking, handsome Dapper Dan loved his awful Uncle Travis, and that he was striking out in the only direction he knew to try and get him back. He was desperation in misdirected slow motion, but his little pistol was pointed at my heart.

I knew what could be next. He would shoot me and Otis would kill him. Maybe I'd survive, and maybe I wouldn't.

I spoke in a kind voice. I said, "You understand as well as I do that threatening us with a pistol won't help you find your uncle if we don't know where he is. Believe me, we don't know where he is."

Dan heaved a sigh and tightened his mouth in resignation.

I said, "Accept my apology for hitting you, holster your weapon, and let's start fresh without anyone getting hurt. Okay?"

He lowered his pistol and then went stiff as the door opened. Henry walked into the room, saw the guns, and pulled his.

"Who's that?" Dan said, louder than he should have.

I said, "It's okay, Henry. We're just getting something settled."

Henry moved into the room, and Dan again pointed his pistol at me.

I said. "Otis, put it down, will you? And Henry, step back a little. Put your pistol away and give us some breathing room."

Henry and Otis didn't put their weapons away, but they moved so they seemed less threatening.

Dan said, "The door," because he had to readjust to the door being open and having an audience of nurses.

"Don't worry about that. Let's finish what we started," I said. "You were putting your pistol away…"

Before anything else could happen, Jim, my one hundred ten pound German shepherd, rushed into the room and pounced on Dapper Dan. The young guy squeezed off a wild shot into the ceiling and hit his head on the bedstead on his way to the floor.

Jim landed on top of Dan, and was snarling in his unconscious face until Henry pulled him away.

The nurses who had been chasing Jim ran into the room, both talking at once. They rushed to Dan, thinking he'd been shot. I looked over at Otis. He was laughing.

Lee, arriving for our supper date, came into the room

with his pistol drawn. "Was there a shot fired in here?" he asked.

"It's okay," I told Lee. "Nothing to worry about."

Otis said, "You should've seen her, Lee. She talked that kid out of his pistol. Missy, the peacemaker."

The nurses found that Dan was alive. "He may have a concussion. He has a recent wound at another place on his head."

I could've taken credit for the earlier wound, but I didn't.

"Let's get him to Emergency," the nurse said.

Lee saw Jim and said, "My god! Where'd he come from?"

Henry released my big boy and he rose up, put his paws on my shoulders, and licked my face.

A nurse said to Henry, "We've told you before. Get that dog out of here before we call the police."

"I *am* the police," Lee said to the nurse. And to Henry, he said, "You're under arrest."

"Never happen, copper," Henry said to Lee in a voice he'd heard on a radio show.

Otis said, "You want me to shoot him, Hank?"

"Come on," I said to Lee. "Let's go dancing. I can't take any more of this."

As we walked out into a hospital corridor alive with curious onlookers, Lee said, "Is he going?"

Jim was trotting along beside us.

"Do you want to tell him he can't?"

"He has to ride in back," Lee said.

"Sure he does," I said.

Lee took my hand and the crowd parted for us.

Some facts about the author from the author:

ROBERT FATE is my pen name. The name on my birth certificate is Robert Fate Bealmear.

I'm a Marine Corps veteran who lived in Paris, studied at the Sorbonne, and can mangle the French language with the best of them. I worked as an oilfield rough neck on a Texaco rig in Northeastern Oklahoma and a TV cameraman in Oklahoma City, jobs not as dissimilar as you might think. I was a fashion model in New York City for a few years to earn a living while I wrote a stage play that never sold. I was a project manager and later a sales exec in Las Vegas after working as a chef in a Los Angeles restaurant, where Gourmet Magazine asked for my Gingerbread recipe—actually, it was my grandmother's recipe. Along the way, I owned a company that airbrushed flowers on silk for the garment industry, and then I wrote scripts for the soap opera *Search For Tomorrow*. With the support and encouragement of a good friend, I produced an independent feature film. As a Hollywood special effects technician, I won an Academy Award for Technical Achievement. Except for the bad parts, I've always thought of life as an enjoyable challenge.

I live in Los Angeles with my wife Fern, a ceramic artist. Our daughter Jenny is a sophomore at USC. We have a dog, four cats, and a turtle named Pharrell.

Website is www.robertfate.com

Email address is robert-fate@sbcglobal.net

Drop me a line.

Robert Fate